"Mrs. Pentland? I should like a word with you, if you please."

Diana stopped, her heart thumping. "Yes, Mr. Lambert?"

"May I ask what you are doing in Brandham?"

"I am staying with Mr. and Mrs. Turner," she said coldly.

"You know very well what I am asking. What is your ulterior motive?"

Diana did not answer.

"Are you after money?" enquired Henry Lambert disagreeably. "Or have you simply come to make trouble?"

But the trouble had already begun...

Fawcett Crest Books
by Sheila Bishop:

LUCASTA
THE RULES OF MARRIAGE
A SPEAKING LIKENESS

A
SPEAKING
LIKENESS

SHEILA
BISHOP

FAWCETT CREST • NEW YORK

PART ONE

The Love Child

I

A grave-looking man at the bank explained the financial situation to Diana Pentland. She understood him easily; there was not much to understand. Coming out into the mercantile bustle of the streets around Charing Cross, her first thought was that she had better walk back to her lodgings. She could not afford to take a hackney. She crossed the road, keeping her wits about her and a wary eye on the fast coach to Brighton which was just leaving the Golden Cross.

At the top of Whitehall she paused. There was King Charles, remote and aloof, riding above the populace, and some way further down, equally statuesque, the two mounted sentries on duty outside the Horse Guards. She had gazed at that building with considerable awe six years ago, when she and Oliver had come to London on their wedding tour. In the long war against Bonaparte, the schemes and decisions of the powerful beings in the Horse

Guards were of vital importance to a junior officer in a line regiment and his young bride. . . . The war still dragged on but scarcely affected her now.

You can't stand here moping, Diana told herself briskly. Which was the best way back to Hans Town? Up the Mall, skirting St. James's Park, across Green Park, and then along the edge of Hyde Park to Knightsbridge.

Having chosen her route, Diana set out, walking rather fast. She was very slender with fine, small bones; this made her seem taller than she actually was, and now, in her deep mourning, she looked almost a wraith, yet she moved so swiftly and gracefully that many people stared after her as she passed. The heavy black veil over her bonnet hid not only her grief, but her fine eye and brilliant complexion, and discouraged the sort of men who might otherwise have accosted her. She would have been grateful for this if she had thought about it, but her mind was elsewhere.

What was she to do? How were they to live? She had no one to advise her. Unprotected, she was not alone, thank God, for there was her precious little Susannah to love her and be loved, and to remind her of Oliver, yet the existence of a three-year-old daughter made her problems far greater.

Diana Bonnington had grown up in Chester where her father was an architect. After his death, when she was thirteen, she and her mother had continued to live in a good style (and perhaps a little too extravagantly), keeping open house and especially popular with the young officers of the garrison, whom kind Mrs. Bonnington treated as though they were a large family of nephews. Oliver Pentland had been a particular favourite. He was an orphan; all his family, he said cheerfully and without self-pity, were killed either by the French or by the Indian climate. He and Diana had fallen in love when she was eighteen. Their friends and connections in Chester had thought it wildly imprudent of Mrs. Bonnington to let her young and very pretty daughter throw herself away on a penniless ensign; perhaps she had been anxious to see Diana settled as soon as possible because she guessed her own life was ending. And there was not a great deal of money left when she died. Although Diana missed her mother very much, she was certainly happy with Oliver, following the drum and living in the closed circle of his brother-officers and their families as the regiment moved about England during the next six years. The husbands chafed a little because they longed to go and have a crack at Bonaparte; their wives hoped secretly that they would never be sent.

It was odd, Diana reflected, how the things one dreaded most often came out differently in the end. The week before the regiment was ordered to the Peninsular, Oliver went down with a fever which the doctors diagnosed as a rare disease he had picked up in the East. They recognised the symptoms but could not cure them. The regiment had sailed for Portugal without him, the wives and children scattered, mostly returning to familiar neighbourhoods where they belonged, and Diana stayed on in Deal to nurse her dying husband. The anguish of the next six months was so great that she dared not look back on it. When everything was finally over, her only remaining wish was to escape from the place where she had been so miserable. At first she could not think where to go. She did not want to return to Chester, had not even written to her cousins there to tell them Oliver was ill. They had not approved of her marriage, and though she was too generous to bear a grudge, she was also too independent to sponge on them. Besides, Chester was such a long way off. And her closest friend among the regimental wives was in Scotland, which was further still. Then she thought of Mrs. Barridge and her comfortable rooms in Hans Town. Mrs. Barridge had been letting lodgings for twenty years; Oliver had stayed there with his parents when he was a child, and he had taken Diana there on several leaves, when they had come up to enjoy the London shops and theatres. Mrs. Barridge was an old friend, and she had welcomed poor Mrs. Pentland and sweet little Miss Sukey into her best rooms on terms which could barely cover their board.

I cannot trade on her good nature indefinitely, thought Diana, stopping suddenly and annoying an old gentleman who cannoned into her from behind. And I can't offer her any more because I haven't got it. The man at the bank had told her how Oliver's very small capital was invested, and she realised that the income from this and her own modest inheritance would not be enough to keep her and Sukey housed and fed. I shall have to find work, she decided, walking indomitably on and refusing to be frightened. I wonder if I could become a dressmaker, or teach in a school. The February morning looked bleak through the depressing film of her black veil, yet there was a crisp tingle in the air; she was sorry now that her senses had not been more alive to it. She had come the whole way back without noticing the austere winter beauty of the three parks.

She crossed Sloane Street, took one side turning and another, and came to the neat terrace where Mrs. Barridge had her tall brick house. It was one of the less imposing of these new streets, respectable if not precisely fashionable. You might see quite a number of private carriages here of an evening. At this hour there was hardly anyone about; the only unexpected sight was a rounded shape, seen through the barred pattern of some area railings, which turned into a woman slumped on a doorstep. She must be drunk, thought Diana, surprised. Some parts of London were full of wretched men and women stupefied by cheap gin: they were not expected in Sloane Place, and most of the inhabitants would be very much shocked.

As she drew nearer, Diana changed her mind. The crouched figure was at once too still and too taut for any of the stages of drunkenness, this was someone in acute pain. Hurrying forward she was aware of other inconsistencies, a thick winter pelisse of the softest, most expensive cloth, a fur muff dropped in the dirt.

"What is the matter? Can I help you?"

The sufferer lifted her head, displaying the small round bonnet and plump unfinished face of a very young girl. In this young face the eyes were blurred with pain and terror.

"My dear, you are feeling very ill!" exclaimed Diana. "Tell me what the matter is."

"It will pass in a minute," whispered the girl.

"I hope it may, but you will make yourself worse sitting on that cold step. Let me take you to my lodgings; I am staying in that house on the corner and you can rest comfortably there until you feel more the thing."

Unprotesting, the girl allowed Diana to help her up. She was exceptionally tall; one day she might be what was called a fine woman, and at her present age she was still so sheathed in her puppy-fat that they had walked some yards before Diana discovered something else about her. Quickening her pace, Diana rapped urgently on Mrs. Barridge's front door.

It was opened by Mrs. Barridge in person; she had taken charge of Sukey while Diana went to see her bankers, and now held up the laughing child to greet her mother.

"Here's Mama come home again! Are you going to tell her what we've got for dinner?"

She broke off staring at the stranger.

Diana gave Sukey a quick kiss, and told her to run and talk to Peggy in the kitchen, making pantomime faces meanwhile at Mrs. Barridge. She steered her visitor into her private parlour and sat down in front of the fire.

"Now don't worry. I'll be back directly."

She returned to the narrow hall, where Mrs. Barridge was alone, having got rid of Sukey.

"What is wrong with your friend, Mrs. Pentland? She looks to be very unwell, poor young lady."

"She's not my friend. I found her sitting on a doorstep and she is just about to be confined."

"You must be mistaken!" exclaimed Mrs. Barridge. She was a gaunt female with a severe expression imperfectly concealing a soft heart. "The girl's too young, and a lady, anyone can see. And even if she is—good heavens, you do not mean immediately?"

"I'm afraid so." After six years in a society of young married couples, Diana was a good judge.

They went into the parlour. There was a bright coal fire, and the girl had unbuttoned her pelisse. Diana and Mrs. Barridge exchanged glances.

"Yes, you are right," muttered the landlady in a glum aside.

"It was very kind of you to bring me in here, ma'am," said the girl in a light, pretty, well-bred voice. "I am quite recovered now, and I must not take up any more of your time."

"Where did you propose to go? I think you would be very unwise to leave this house, and you certainly will not get far. How often are you having the pains?"

"I don't understand," the girl lied weakly. "It—it was nothing but a little stitch."

"My dear, you need not be shy with us. We have both been married."

As soon as she had spoken Diana could have bitten back the words. The girl blushed painfully and began to cry.

"But I am not married," she sobbed. Her ringless hands went up to cover her face. "Oh, what can I do? You will turn me out into the street and I shall die!"

"Stuff and nonsense," said Mrs. Barridge. "We'll take care of you, miss, don't you fret. Mrs. Pentland will assist you upstairs while I fetch some old sheets."

The girl was pathetically grateful. She told them her baby was not due for another three weeks and the first onset of labour pains had taken her by surprise. The next half-hour was very busy. Diana managed to have one private exchange with her landlady.

"I am sorry to have given you all this trouble. Perhaps I should not have brought her here."

"Of course you were right to bring her. And it's lucky the Murrays have written to postpone their visit. The bedroom is free, and there is no one here to pry."

Mrs. Barridge generally let her rooms for short periods to officers and their families. Just now, in February, there was a lull.

"She tells me she is not quite seventeen," said Diana. "Do you think we ought to call in a midwife?"

"She seems healthy enough, and I've delivered babies before now. Only I wish you would try to find out, ma'am, who she is and where she comes from. A fine thing it would be if she was to die on our hands and we didn't know her name."

Diana went into the clean, cold bedroom where the unknown girl was looking very apprehensive, though not experiencing any spasms of pain at present. Remarking brightly that they had not been properly introduced, Diana gave her own name and waited.

"I am Elizabeth—Smith." After a distinct hesitation. "If you would please call me Eliza, ma'am."

Very well, thought Diana: it would be absurd to call you Miss Smith. Everything about Eliza, her voice, her manner, the fine materials and exquisite stitching of her clothes and their absolute simplicity, suggested the highest social setting. Not mere gentility and certainly not mere money, but the highest combination of both had gone to the making of this unhappy child who had been wandering in the streets, about to give birth to an illegitimate baby.

What are her family about, Diana wondered indignantly. Don't they know? Has she managed to hide her condition all this time? It would have been just possible, with her rather massive build. There was an alternative: that she had left home and was living with her lover.

"Your friends must be wondering where you are. Would you like me to send a message?"

"Oh no, thank you," in a frightened voice.

So she was not with a lover.

"My dear child, you may want to run away and hide, but if you disappear there will be a search-party out looking for you and perhaps a great scandal—"

"No one is going to search for me, Mrs. Pentland, I promise you. I have been staying in London with my aunt and she thinks I have gone home today. Only I didn't go, I sent my maid with a letter to Mama, saying I was invited to stay with my friend Aurelia, who lives in—well, that doesn't matter. I thought she would know what to do, because she has several married sisters, only when I went to the house, Aurie had been sent down to their place in Devonshire to prevent her catching the measles. All her little brothers are full of the measles. It is so stupid of them. So I had nowhere to go. I was obliged to leave my trunk in the hired carriage—I told the driver some story —and I walked about for hours and hours. I suppose that is what brought on those hateful pains a month too early."

Eliza screwed up her face; the pains were starting again and she could not answer any more questions. At least they need not worry about her being missed, or fear the arrival of a posse of Bow Street Runners in Sloane Place.

Eliza had a short and easy labour, made easier by her good health and stamina. Whatever the folly that had landed her in this fix, she had plenty of physical courage. Good breeding stock, thought Diana; that was how Oliver's colonel would have put it.

Soon after nine in the evening the age-old miracle was repeated once more: at one moment there were three people in the lamplit bedroom and at the next there were four—Diana, Mrs. Barridge, the exhausted young mother and a red, furious, bawling boy.

Mrs. Barridge cut the cord and attended to Eliza. Diana bathed the baby and dressed him in some hastily aired clothes that Mrs. Barridge had unearthed from a box in the attic during the afternoon. At first glance she thought he was perfectly made, though small. When she was manoeuvring one of his little curled-up arms into the sleeve of a flannel shirt, she studied his hands. Babies' hands always fascinated her; they were like tiny pink starfish. The little finger of the new baby's left hand was short of one joint; the tiny oval nail was there, as on all the other fingers, but there were only two joints instead of three. She glanced at the other hand. No, that was properly shaped. It was not a serious malformation and could hardly signify.

"Do you want to see your fine boy?" she asked.

"He's nothing to me. Don't bring him near." Eliza turned her head away.

Later in the evening, however, she said she might as well take a look at him. A long drawer from the tallboy had been turned into a makeshift cradle. Diana picked the white bundle out of its snug nest and put it in Eliza's arms She saw the expression of wonder and tenderness chase away the dull indifference as Eliza gazed at her son. She began to unwind the shawl, freeing the comfortably pinioned arms that came wavering out because he did not know what to do with them. Eliza snatched at his left hand with a cry of dismay.

"It's such a very slight thing," said Diana, knowing

how dreadfully a mother minded the hint of any deformity. "I doubt if anyone will notice it. And there is nothing else wrong, I assure you."

Eliza was not listening. She was still gazing at the baby with the tears running down her cheeks. Diana caught the faint, astonished whisper.

"He's the image of Henry."

And then a flood of weeping.

II

So the baby's father was called Henry, was he? A man with a congenital deformity of one finger, and a deformity of conscience also if he could seduce a girl of sixteen and leave her to face the consequences. That was all Diana could deduce about Eliza's lover in the next few days, for Eliza was recovering rapidly and she had become cautious about everything she said.

Mrs. Barridge heard of a suitable wet-nurse in the riverside village of Chelsea. Martha's husband was a seaman, and she was glad to bring her own flourishing baby and settle herself in the warm kitchen at Sloane Place. She had ample milk for two, so perhaps it was reasonable that she ate enough for six. Sukey Pentland was delighted with the two babies who were now living in the house, she looked on them as very superior dolls and kept wanting to play with them.

On the day she paid her weekly rent, Diana tried to

add something towards the upkeep of Eliza and her en-
cumbrances. Mrs. Barridge refused to take a penny of
this, and they had an absurd half-quarrel, each knowing
the other could not afford to be out of pocket.

"Though I fancy I'm better placed than you are,
ma'am, if you'll excuse my saying so," declared Mrs.
Barridge finally. "You've got your little girl to think of,
and I'm on my own now and very well able to care for
myself. What I wish you would do is try to find out from
Miss Eliza who her friends are and who is to have charge
of that poor little mite. She'll take it better, coming from
a lady like yourself, and closer to her own age."

Diana did not feel they were close in age, as she sat
sewing in Eliza's room that afternoon. She was hemming
a robe for the baby and had pulled her chair close to the
window to get the best of the failing light. Her woolen
dress was oppressive—what a suffocating colour black
was. She wore a white cap which completely covered her
hair, and over that a small hood of black silk with a lace
border, this being the correct indoor wear for widows.
The stark black and white, drawn sharply against the
skin, was generally unbecoming, and was meant to be; it
did not occur to her that her regular features, clear complexion, and violet blue eyes, in that severe frame, had
the timeless beauty often seen in the face of a nun.

Eliza was propped up in bed. She had short fair hair
and an open, pleasant face, now drawn with strain. The
baby slept benignly in the mahogany drawer.

Diana knew it would be useless to ask a direct question, so she tried an oblique approach.

"I expect you enjoy staying in town with your aunt?"

(What a stupid thing to have said, Diana reflected. Eliza's latest visit to London could have been nothing short
of a nightmare.)

However, she answered quite naturally. "My aunt is
very vague and short-sighted, and she is supposed to be a

bluestocking. All she cares for is music and philosophy. I used to go to the shops with my maid, or sometimes to visit my friend Aurelia. Of course I was not invited to any balls or parties because I am not yet out!"

Not yet out! Diana thought she had never heard a remark that was at once so inept and so pathetic.

Eliza shifted restlessly. "I came up to stay with Aunt so that I could go to the dentist. I told Mama I had toothache, just so that I could get away from home. And thank heaven I did."

"Yes, I understand that. You don't want your parents to know what has happened. But my dear Eliza, surely they love you very much and will be prepared to make allowances. You should begin to think of going home. And you will have to write to them soon in any case, even if you don't tell the whole truth at once, or they will start worrying that you are ill."

"There is only Mama, and she never supposes anyone is ill except herself," said Eliza with a certain bitterness. "Oh dear, I should not have said that. She has had such a sad life."

Diana made a mental vow: *Never, never will I let my troubles get the better of me, and run the risk of Sukey saying something like that, in similar circumstances, twelve or thirteen years from now.*

"Have you any brothers or sisters?"

"I have one brother, older than I—he came of age this year. He is very serious and good and clever. And handsome too. He and I have always got on famously."

This sounded more promising.

"Don't you think that perhaps if you confided in him—"

"No, no!" cried Eliza. "I could never tell him what I have done, and if he knew there was a baby, he would be so disgusted and mortified, he would never speak to me again. I think he would hate me. He and Mama are not the sort of people who—they are not passionate and wicked like me." She broke into a paroxysm of tears and through her sobs Diana caught one more fragment of information: ". . . His great friend, which makes it so much worse. God knows what he would do. . . ."

If the villainous Henry was her brother's friend, he must be quite young and a gentleman. (Eliza had not fallen a victim to a handsome groom or footman, a possibility which had crossed Diana's mind.) So why had he not married her? Any inequality of fortune would surely have been overlooked, in the circumstances. Probably he had simply been amusing himself, and the feelings of the high-minded brother, if he found out, might well be imagined.

Nothing more could be said at present.

As Eliza grew stronger she got up and dressed, came downstairs and passed the time staring into the parlour fire or reading Diana's library books. She cried a good deal, but this was a natural after-effect of childbirth, and she seemed to be living inside a shell of unreality, for she made no plans and never spoke of money, except to remark that she had only eight shillings in her purse. Not that she was ungrateful. She continually thanked Diana and Mrs. Barridge for being so good to her. By this she meant their uncensorious kindness toward a fallen woman, which was how the poor child saw herself. The idea that she was a burden on the household never entered her head.

"How should it?" remarked Diana. "She comes from a wealthy family, we've always guessed that, and I don't suppose she ever heard anyone speak of the expense of having visitors to stay for several weeks. She is not selfish, simply ignorant."

"I expect you are right," agreed Mrs. Barridge thoughtfully.

It was a very fine morning, and Diana took Sukey to

Hyde Park. Sukey loved to watch the prancing horses in Rotten Row, and on this particular morning Diana took a new interest in the riders. Those dashing men and elegant women with their easy manners and confident voices, all recognised members of the *Ton*: were any of them acquainted with Eliza and her family? What a pity there was no way of finding out.

When they got back to Sloane Place, the door was opened to them by Mrs. Barridge, who announced dramatically, "She's gone!"

"Who's gone? You don't mean Miss Eliza?—Run along to Peggy, my love, there's a good girl—Where has she gone?"

"I don't know. I was down in the basement, speaking to Peggy about the cold mutton, when I heard the front door slam. She's walked out of the house and I greatly fear she doesn't mean to come back."

"Why not? She hasn't taken the baby?" asked Diana, her heart contracting with a sudden dread.

"No, he's with Martha."

"Then she has simply gone for a stroll in the fresh air. It may do her good."

"I hope so. But I feel bound to tell you, ma'am, that I had a talk with our young lady which may have been the cause—I meant it for the best," said Mrs. Barridge, looking very red and uncomfortable. "Only I may have done more harm than good, and you will be angry with me."

"Dear Mrs. Barridge, I'm sure I shan't be anything of the sort."

"It was on account of what you said earlier." The landlady followed Diana into the parlour. "That Miss Eliza has probably spent her whole life among people of means. She must know that I let lodgings to earn my bread—no one could fail to understand that—but I thought she might well have mistaken your situation, thinking you to be a lady of considerable fortune, and I found this was exactly the case when I mentioned quite casually that things were very difficult for you at present. She was quite overcome. She seems to have imagined you had a house of your own somewhere in the country; of course she had noticed that you do not go out in society or receive callers, but she put this down to your being in mourning. She understood at once that she ought not to go on accepting her board and lodging from either of us—not that I grudge her my spare room while it is standing empty, or the run of her teeth for a week or two longer. I simply wanted to force her hand, so that she would feel obliged to apply to her family. I didn't mean her to run off without a word. Now you can tell me what a foolish old meddler I have been!"

"No, of course not," said Diana hastily. She did feel that Mrs. Barridge had been unwise to attack Eliza in her present state of mind, but it would have been useless and unkind to say so.

"I hope she may not go into the Serpentine," Mrs. Barridge was saying in a fit of remorse. "Or jump off Westminster Bridge."

"Not in broad daylight. She wouldn't have a chance."

"That's very true. Perhaps she means to decamp and leave us to provide for the baby. She could go back to her family, knowing that neither you nor I would turn him over to the parish."

"I don't believe she would abandon him without a word," said Diana.

Yet she felt an unexpected surge of—was it hope? Surely not. One could not wish Eliza to behave so unnaturally. It was the idea of having to keep the baby that lit a spark in Diana's heart. The strange arrival in her life of Eliza, and the birth of this little unwanted boy, had brought her a distraction from her own sorrows, and several times in the past fortnight she had thought of suggesting that she should take him off Eliza's hands. She suspected that Eliza was hoping for this. She had told herself severely that she must resist the temptation to do anything so mad. Here she was, wondering whether she could earn enough by teaching or dressmaking to provide for herself and Sukey; how could she possibly take on another child, and a boy at that? A girl could be educated at home; and if she had a good disposition and good manners she would grow up the equal of other girls, even if she had no fortune. A boy had to be sent to school and into a profession; it was out of the question. . . . Unless Eliza had actually abandoned him, for then one would feel justified in keeping him, to save him from the alternative.

Diana went and looked at the baby, Martha had returned him to his mahogany crib. He was sleeping blissfully; his right hand (the perfect one) had worked out of the shawl and was pressed against his ear. He looked very tiny. Diana thought of the workhouse children, sad little unloved drudges, and of that even more pathetic tribe, the thousands of children who wandered homeless in the poorer London streets, slept in rat-infested lairs and were driven into crime and vice without knowing right from wrong.

"My little treasure, I won't let those things happen to you," she whispered, with an anguish of compassion so acute that it compared with the physical pain she had felt in giving birth to Sukey. It seemed as though a real bond now existed between her and this stranger's child.

By half-past four Mrs. Barridge was again talking about Westminster Bridge. Diana stood at her bedroom window, looking out over Sloane Place, which was quite a short street, and hoping to see the figure of a tall girl in a brown pelisse. She did not pay much attention to the smart town chaise that had just turned in from the direction of Knightsbridge, until it drew up immediately outside the house. It was a private carriage, luxuriously appointed and well-sprung. The horses were as glossy as the paintwork; every separate piece of brass glittered on the harness and on the lamp fittings. The side panel bore a family crest, too small to make out from above, and, unmistakably, a coronet.

A footman jumped down from the box and banged on Mrs. Barridge's front door. Then he helped someone to alight from the carriage. It was Eliza.

Diana ran down into the hall. By the time she got there, the door was shut and Eliza was inside, being made much of by Mrs. Barridge and the maid, and assuring them that she was not in the least hungry, cold or tired.

When she was alone in the parlour with Diana, she said, "I'm sorry if I caused you any alarm, Mrs. Pentland. You see, I had to go out—I have only now begun to realise that I must not be imposing on your good nature forever."

She did not say "I know you are too poor to support me any longer," and Diana recognised this kind of delicacy as the proof of a good upbringing. Eliza was pink-cheeked and bright-eyed, almost pretty, and she seemed none the worse for her long absence.

"We were a little afraid that you might overtax your strength. Would it be indiscreet to ask where you have been?"

"Where I should have gone in the first place: to the person who was most likely to protect me. And he has been so wonderfully kind." Eliza turned away, pretending to examine a rather bad print of Garrick as Richard III. She was obviously in a state of deep emotion. "I did not know he loved me so much. Of course Mama was always set against him, and I thought—from the way he behaved—that he must be quite heartless. I did him the greatest injury."

He's going to marry her, thought Diana, with a generous glow of pleasure. So she was quite unprepared for Eliza's next announcement.

"He is going to see to everything—find a good home for the baby where he will be properly taken care of, and make some provision for his future—and I shall be able to go home as if nothing has happened. No one will ever know. I shall be able to come out in the spring as I was always supposed to do."

Diana heard her in amazement. Was this the limit of the young man's kindness and love for which she seemed so abjectly grateful? How could any girl be satisfied with such treatment? Then a totally new idea sprang into view: perhaps Eliza's lover was already married? That would explain a great deal and Diana wondered why she had not thought of it before. And a married man, however badly he had behaved in the first place, could not do any more for Eliza and her child than he was offering to do now.

"How is my little boy?" asked Eliza casually. "I hope he has been good."

"Perfectly good all day. He is a very contented baby."

"I have decided on his name. He is to be called Henry."

Eliza spoke rather complacently, as though bestowing some rare gift. It was the only one, thought Diana, that she seemed willing to bestow on her son. She was longing to be rid of him, so that she could return to the life of a pampered young girl that he, poor little creature, had unwittingly interrupted. One ought not to condemn her. She was very young. Too young, perhaps, to experience the true feelings of a mother.

III

The following morning another carriage stopped outside the house in Sloane Place. It was not quite such a glorious conveyance but extremely respectable, the sort that could be hired from the best livery stables. A letter was delivered, addressed to Mrs. Pentland in an elderly, learned hand. Diana opened it with eager curiosity.

> Lincoln's Inn Fields.
> 20th February.

My Dear Madam,

A valued client of mine has been given your name by the Young Lady at present residing in the same house as yourself, and to whom you have shown such unexampled kindness. I should esteem it a favour if you would do me the honour of calling on me in the near future. If it is agreeable, you might care to come this morning in the chaise which brings you this letter. The coachman has been told to await your instructions.

I remain, my dear madam,
    Your obliged servant,
        E. Caversham.

"An attorney, from his address," said Mrs. Barridge, to whom Diana showed the letter. Eliza was still in bed. "I wonder what he wants."

"To find out how much of the young lady's history is known to me and to ask me to keep my mouth shut. I might as well go at once—if it would not be a great nuisance for you to take care of Sukey for me?"

Mrs. Barridge was delighted to take care of Sukey. Diana put on her black bonnet and pelisse and set out in the respectable carriage. Another possible reason for the lawyer's letter had struck her immediately, but she would not allow herself to dwell on it, in case she was disappointed.

When she arrived at the house in the famous legal square, she was ushered into a fine room, panelled in the fashion of two centuries before, where two middle-aged men were seated behind a polished table.

"My dear ma'am, how good of you to come so promptly," said the elder, moving forward to greet her. "Will you take a chair near the fire? A cold morning, is it not? I am Mr. Caversham, and this is my associate, Mr. Wood."

The second man merely rose and made Diana a slight bow. When Mr. Caversham had settled her comfortably, he returned to his place behind the table and began to speak in measured periods.

"My client is particularly anxious that I should express his deep sense of gratitude and obligation for your kindness to the young lady, whom it will be convenient to refer to as Miss Elizabeth. . . ."

Only it is not convenient, Diana could not help thinking, to talk about two people whose names must never be revealed and whose connection is so decidedly improper.

And how is this old bumblebee going to speak of the baby? Any stranger who came into the room might really wonder what I am being thanked for.

She caught a swift glance from the younger lawyer, and with it the impression that he knew just what she was thinking and agreed with her. He was about forty, a fair, broad-shouldered man with undistinguished features and very shrewd blue eyes. Diana looked demurely down at her black, gloved hands as they lay in her lap.

Mr. Caversham was now speaking of the unfortunate infant. (Yes, of course: he would call Baby Henry that.) Then there was a slight pause, and he began again, in a less pontifical voice, to ask Diana various questions about her own circumstances. She had been prepared for this and replied quite frankly. After a while, however, it struck her that the questions were taking an odd turn. What was it to Mr. Caversham or Mr. Wood how long Oliver had been ill in the lodgings at Deal or when she had last written to her mother's cousins in Chester? She felt that his intrusive prying must have something to do with the obliterating secrecy with which they wanted to surround Eliza's lapse. They were trying to find out exactly who Diana's friends were and whom she might gossip to. This annoyed her and she answered rather shortly. Mr. Wood fidgeted with the papers in front of him. Mr. Caversham brought the catechism to an end.

"Would you excuse us for a few minutes, ma'am?"

The two men got up and went solemnly out of the room, Mr. Wood holding the door open for his senior. Diana was left in a state of suspended animation.

She did not have to wait long. When the lawyers came back, Mr. Caversham began: "Mrs. Pentland, I have been empowered by our client to ask whether you would consider taking Miss Elizabeth's infant son and bringing him up as your own. He would make you a very generous allowance, from which you and your daughter would also benefit."

Diana was so glad to receive such an offer that she heard only the gist of what he was saying. She accepted at once, adding, "It will be good for my little girl to have another child brought up with her, and I would have liked to take him for that reason, and for his own sake, without any talk of money. But as you know, my means are so straitened that I must accept to the allowance."

Mr. Caversham was about to reply when Mr. Wood spoke for the first time, in a clear, incisive tone. "Forgive me, ma'am: I think you may not have quite understood what Mr. Caversham was suggesting. Our client does not wish you merely to bring up the boy *with* your own child but *as* your own child. To give him your name and pass him off as your son."

"Pass him off?" she repeated.

"You have been asked a great many questions which you found impertinent—I noticed that and I don't blame you. Now you can see their object. If you were to let it be thought that you have just become the mother of a posthumous child, is there anyone among your friends or family connections who would be either scandalised or offended or frankly incredulous?"

"No one," she said slowly, thinking this over. "I was so cut off during my husband's illness. All the same, I am not sure that I want to—I shall have to consider—"

"Perhaps," said Mr. Caversham, "you are reluctant to give your late husband's name to an infant whose antecedents are shrouded in a veil of anonymity. Let me assure you, ma'am, that he is descended from two very ancient and distinguished families, even though he was born—"

"On the wrong side of the blanket," put in Mr. Wood, who obviously had no patience with his colleague's sonorous phrases. "My dear sir, I don't think Mrs. Pentland cares about noble lineage or best blankets; she simply wants to know that the child has some hope of growing up sane, healthy and reasonably moral, in spite of the folly of his parents."

Mr. Caversham glared at him. He seemed not only indignant but personally affronted. Diana thought he was a man whose reverence for his noble client probably outweighed every other feeling. Mr. Wood, on the other hand, looked as though he thought very little of the aristocracy, even if he was not above making money out of them.

In fact, the baby's actual descent mattered as little to her as his being illegitimate. She had simply jibbed at the idea of giving Oliver's name to someone else's son. But would Oliver himself have objected? He had been generous with all his possessions, and she suddenly had an odd impression that she could hear his voice saying, "Go on, Di. Let the little fellow have my name. He needs it and no one else does."

"Very well," she said to the lawyers. "I am prepared to do what your client asks."

They both seemed so pleased that she could not help being flattered.

Mr. Caversham got down quite briskly to practical details. They proposed to rent a small house in a quiet country district where the air was good, and where she and Sukey and the baby could live in what Messrs. Caversham and Wood described as simple comfort, which sounded to Diana like absolute luxury. Her allowance would be paid quarterly. Later on, arrangements would be made for the boy's schooling. Diana had to admit that Mr. Caversham's client was prepared to pay handsomely for his indiscretion.

"We had thought of Essex as a suitable country," said Mr. Caversham. "There is one condition I have not mentioned, by the way. If you should ever think of removing to another part of the country, you must consult me first. There are certain places—not very many—that our client wishes you to avoid."

Diana saw the good sense in this. Once she had taken charge of the little boy, the last people she would wish to meet were his natural parents.

"You have no servants of your own at present, I understand? That is a good thing. Servants gossip so. No one in your new home must have any reason to suppose you are not the child's mother."

"What about the wet nurse?" asked Mr. Wood. "You'll have to take her."

"Yes, but I need not keep her more than a week or so. She will not have time to chatter. I shall buy a goat."

"Will that serve the purpose?" Mr. Wood sounded really interested.

"Certainly. Goat's milk is the finest nourishment for a young child."

Mr. Caversham looked so horrified by this exchange that Diana could hardly keep from laughing. Apparently they had shocked his nice sense of propriety.

Reminding herself of the real seriousness behind the whole business, she said, "I appreciate that it is necessary to avoid gossip and speculation. But how much may I say to Miss Elizabeth? Is she to know where her son is going?"

"We shall let her know that you have agreed to keep him," Mr. Caversham replied. "That will be assurance enough, for she has the greatest admiration of you, ma'am. She will not know where you are to live. And you need not fear any distressing scenes. By the time you return to Sloane Place, Miss Elizabeth will have left."

"Already?" Diana was taken aback.

"A sudden break seemed kindest," said Mr. Wood. "And she ought to go home immediately. Every day she remains in Sloane Place, the greater the risk that her mother and aunt will compare notes and realise she is missing."

Which was perfectly true. Eliza's lover was determined to avoid a scandal, and he had some very efficient agents to help him.

PART TWO

An Offer of Marriage

I

━━

"Come quickly, Mama!" cried Sukey Pentland, running across the little lawn at Palfreys as fast as her six-year-old legs would bring her. "Hop's got under the strawberry net and I can't pull him out nohow!"

"Dear me," said Diana placidly. "What a terrible fellow he is for getting into scrapes."

She put down her trowel and followed Sukey round the side of the house to the patch of kitchen garden. Between a clump of gooseberry bushes and a row of beans, a fine crop of hautboys had been thickly strawed and covered with a low net. Under the net, on his hands and knees, was Master Henry Oliver Pentland, now aged three.

He was undoubtedly stuck. One mesh of the net had caught round a button of his pantaloons and another was looped over his ear, but instead of bawling to be rescued, he was very sensibly stuffing himself with strawberries while he had the chance.

"You wicked fellow," said Diana, laughing and disentangling him from the net. He was a slim, agile, wriggling boy, with a pointed face and curly dark hair. One curl, like a tuft of feathers, always fell forward into his eyes, which were hazel green and full of merriment. His mouth at the moment was blood red.

"Torbies," he said unnecessarily.

"Yes, and you've eaten about a pound, by the look of it. You had better go in now to Nancy, both of you: it's time for your rest. And this afternoon we'll walk over to the farm and fetch the butter."

"Neddy come too?"

"Yes, and you can take turns riding him."

"Hurry along, you wicked fellow," said Sukey, grasping Hop's hand and imitating her mother, even to the tone of voice.

Diana was sometimes afraid that she and Sukey loved Hop so much they would not be able to help spoiling him.

He had been christened Henry because his real mother had wished it, and Oliver because it would have seemed very odd if his adopting mother had not called him after his supposed father. Diana had different reasons for not really wishing to use either name, so she had started calling him Hop after seeing his initials entwined on a christening mug thoughtfully provided by Mr. Wood. He and Mr. Caversham had volunteered to act as godfathers, this being one thing Diana felt unable to ask of her dead husband's friends without telling them the truth. So Caversham and Wood had made all those solemn promises for little Henry Oliver in the parish church at Knightsbridge, and provided suitably handsome gifts—though Diana imagined that these had been paid for by the man she always thought of now (in biting irony and capital letters) as the Noble Client.

She disliked being the pensioner of such a man, even while admitting that his liberality made her life extremely pleasant.

Palfreys was a neat brick building with sash windows and white paintwork, standing alone in half an acre of land, but only a hundred yards from the village street of Great Wickfield. There were four bedrooms, the largest being used as a nursery, as well as a drawing room and dining room, and here Diana had lived for the last three years with Sukey and Hop, a sensible young nurse, a cook, a housemaid and two cats. The garden was full of pinks and lilac, peonies and larkspur. There was a rustic rose arbour and a well-stocked orchard. The heavy gardening was done by a character known as Old Skingle, who harangued his mistress in such a strong Essex drawl that she didn't always know what he was saying. Sukey and Hop had a distressing tendency to talk like Old Skingle.

In a tiny paddock next to the orchard lived Cicely, the goat, whose rich, pure milk had nourished the baby Hop for the first year of his life. They still drank her milk or made cheese from it. This spring Neddy the donkey had been put in there to join her. Diana had been rather nervous about this, but they got on surprisingly well for such notoriously crotchety animals.

She returned to the front garden and went on bedding out the sweet williams. Presently the low iron gate clicked behind her and a voice said, "Good morning, Mrs. Pentland."

Diana stood up. "Good morning, Mr. Brownlees."

"I just happened to be passing and I thought I might look in on you."

It was remarkable how often Diana's landlord just happened to be passing these days.

He was an erect, well-made man of thirty-six, with glossy brown hair and rather serious brown eyes, into which a shy smile crept as he gazed admiringly at Diana.

She had come out of mourning and was wearing a pink gingham dress, with a serviceable apron to keep off the dirt. Her face was protected by a coarse straw bonnet. Framed in this, her skin had a glow of health and her dark blue eyes were brilliant. She peeled off her gardening gloves.

"Shall we go into the arbour? It is too fine to waste time indoors. And may I offer you a glass of madeira? I hardly dare to suggest goat's milk."

Roger Brownlees politely refused any refreshment.

It was pleasant sitting in the arbour. The green branches were covered with clusters of shallow, flat roses, their carmine buds opening into a delicate blush pink. Roger Brownlees began to talk about music, which was an interest he and Diana shared. He had heard that the score of one of Mozart's operas had been adapted for the pianoforte. Would she not like a copy? Then he would enquire at Broadwood's when he was in town.

"You are going to London?"

"To meet my sister and her family who are coming over from Ireland. They will be with me at the Hall for at least six weeks. I hope we shall see a great deal of you while Bella is with me, she has heard so much about you."

"Oh. Has she?"

"You are mentioned in all my letters. How could it be otherwise? I shall start by giving a dinner and I depend on your coming to it. I know you don't dine out as a rule, but this will be a special occasion. I thought I would ask all the Pelhams, as company for Bella's boys and girls, and then afterwards we might have some dancing. It would be quite acceptable where there are so many young people, don't you agree? Only what I really want is to have an opportunity of dancing with you, my dear Mrs. Pentland," explained Mr. Brownlees, looking like a bashful schoolboy.

Taken off her guard, Diana said, "I used to be very fond of dancing. Only I don't think I should—I'm sure it is not proper for widows."

"But that strikes at the very heart of the matter, doesn't it? Surely you don't always intend to remain a widow?"

And before she could reply, Diana found he was making her an impassioned offer of marriage. He had been in love with her for months: he spoke of her beauty, her vivacity, her devotion to her delightful children, her goodness to the poor. He flattered himself that they thought the same way on all serious subjects. If she would allow him the infinite happiness of cherishing and protecting her from now on. . . .

"You must give me time to think, Mr. Brownlees. I am extremely obliged to you, but you have taken me completely by surprise."

Diana felt a perfect fool as she said this. She had no business to be so surprised. A woman who had been married once was supposed to recognise signs and portents, and to know her own mind by the time she received an offer.

Roger Brownlees took all the blame—in a very gentlemanly way. "I ought not to have plunged on before you were ready to listen. Do forgive me for being so clumsy. We need not talk of this again until you feel equal to it."

He rose to leave, seeming almost anxious to get away in case his presence was putting too much strain on her sensibilities. As they reached the gate, he said, "I don't know if there is anyone you could turn to for advice; you have no close relatives, I believe? Jackson has been rector here for twelve years and knows a good deal about me; he would speak as to my character. And naturally I should expect to satisfy your trustees."

Diana did not immediately take in the full meaning of this remark. She watched her landlord and friend—now her suitor—set off towards Great Wickfield Hall, his fine old house at the far end of the village. Then she went back and sat in the rose arbour.

Why hadn't she realised he was in love with her, on the point of proposing? Perhaps because they had met at a time when neither of them seemed at all likely to marry anybody. Diana was still grieving for Oliver and stunned by her loss. And Roger Brownlees' mother had been alive, a difficult, selfish invalid, determined not to be driven out of her old home or share it with a daughter-in-law. Diana had got to know him as a predestined bachelor, and when his mother died, a year ago, she was so accustomed to think of him in this way that she had not taken his admiration seriously.

Now he had actually made her an offer. What was she to do? Could she imagine him as her husband? She was not in love, of course, but one did not expect to marry for love a second time. He was agreeable and kind, a conscientious landlord and magistrate, always busily engaged in managing his property and farming part of it himself. After three years of seclusion, Diana was beginning to feel that she would like a little more scope for her very active disposition. No one would ever supplant Oliver, or make her forget their happy early love, but one was not an Indian widow on a funeral pyre and it was impossible to make life stand still. She was only twenty-seven years old. And it would be good for the children to have the right sort of stepfather.

The children! She was brought up short. If she did decide to marry Roger Brownlees, what was she to tell him about Hop? She now recalled something he had said about her trustees. He received her rent every quarter-day from the Noble Client's grand London lawyers, and of course he thought they were administering her late husband's estate. Diana did not imagine for a moment that he had mistaken her for a rich woman, nor that he was fortune-hunting; all the same, any man who was getting married was bound to take an interest in his bride's finances, especially when there were children by a previous husband. Brownlees would expect to be shown some document—a will or a settlement—to account for the income on which he had seen the Pentlands living very comfortably for the past three years.

Instead, there was nothing to show but her own tiny inheritance, a bunch of letters from the lawyers, agreeing to pay for everything she needed but not explaining how or why, and in the background the shadowy presence of the Noble Client. What would Brownlees make of that? Well, there seemed to be only one thing that anybody could make of it.

Diana began to walk about the lawn. Mr. Caversham and Mr. Wood, those respectable conspirators, had been so eager to protect Eliza and the Client, they had persuaded her to promise she would play the part of Hop's mother, and never give the truth away to a soul, without pointing out that she would be very awkwardly placed if she ever wanted to give another person the right to look into her private concerns.

At that time, so soon after Oliver's death, she would not have cared. She was sure she would never marry again. The lawyers, with their professional experience, ought to have seen further than she did. Now they would have to release her from her promise.

She went into the drawing-room, sat down at her pretty little secretaire, and started to compose a letter.

II

...

Diana had not seen anyone from the attorneys' office
since she had been in Essex. All their business had been
carried on by letter. She wrote regularly to Mr. Caversham, giving news of Hop, which she had been asked to
do—presumably to satisfy the Noble Client. Mr. Caversham answered punctiliously. Every now and then it was
Mr. Wood who replied. His letters were less stiff and he
seemed to take a practical interest in the arrangements at
Palfreys. It was Mr. Wood who had advised her to buy a
donkey, so that she could take the children further afield
than they could walk.

Roger Brownlees had proposed to her on a Monday;
she had written and posted her letter to Mr. Caversham
the same day, and hoped to receive an answer by Thursday. In ten days' time Mr. Brownlees was going to London to meet his relations from Ireland, and then there
was to be an outbreak of dinners and picnics, and if
Diana had not got her own situation clarified by then she
might feel very awkward. She was sure Mrs. O'Hara had
a great many probing questions to ask the designing female who had ensnared her brother.

Only I don't mean to be designing, thought Diana. The design I'm caught up in was arranged by someone else.

Thursday's post brought her a letter from Major and Mrs. Robinson, some old army friends, nothing from Caversham. She felt disappointed and cross.

It was a cheerless morning. The clouds gave off a pale glare. In this part of Essex the land was not dead flat but wide open, without many trees. There was a great deal of sky and not much landscape. The wind blew continually from the east.

Skingle, scything the grass, said it was a nasty old day.

At about one o'clock Nancy was going to take the children to the village, and Diana was at the door to watch them start, when they saw two men approaching the house on foot.

One of them was Joe, from the Red Lion, who was carrying some large, odd-shaped parcels and seemed to be showing the way to his companion, a tall broad-shouldered gentleman in a cutaway coat, light breeches, and well-polished hessians. They turned in at the little gate.

"Why, it's Mr. Wood!" exclaimed Diana.

He came towards her, smiling and saying something about answering her letter in person. He was taller than she remembered.

Hop stood gazing up at him with his mouth open. Mr. Wood looked at him and laughed.

"Well, I know who you are! How do you do, young Henry?"

"Say good morning to your godfather, my love," prompted Diana.

Hop said politely that it was a nasty old day, speaking in the accents of Essex and Jeremiah Skingle. Diana was mortified, but Mr. Wood seemed highly amused.

"Speaks the language like a native, doesn't he? And this tall young lady must be Sukey."

He then gave Joe a shilling and thanked him for acting as a guide. "Just put the parcels in the porch, will you?"

Both children were obviously bursting to know what was in the parcels, and Mr. Wood did not keep them in suspense. Taking out his pocketknife, he said, "We had better cut the string. Toyshop people always tie up everything so securely. One supposes they do it on purpose to tease."

"They come from a toyshop," whispered Sukey ecstatically.

Diana thought with a slight pang that her daughter was going to be disappointed: the toys would be for Hop. But when the layers of paper were folded back they found not only a fine box of oak bricks, but also a beautiful doll with a wax face and two sets of clothes. Her heart warmed towards Mr. Wood.

"How very kind of you," she murmured, over the heads of the children, "to remember Sukey as well."

"I hope it is the right sort of doll. I am not a connoisseur."

The last parcel was flat, containing some sections of coloured canvas, sticks, and string. Hop hardly glanced at them; he was already building a wall with his bricks. Sukey, after staring in silence, said, "It's a kite!"

"How did you know?" Diana asked her. "You've never seen one, have you, Sukey?"

"The boy has one in my picturebook. Oh, Mama, can we fly it now?"

"Not today, my love. Mr. Wood has come all the way from London to see me—"

"I am in no particular hurry, ma'am. And it's just the weather for kite-flying. I have left my chaise at the postinghouse, and ordered dinner there. I could return here afterwards for our discussion, if you don't object."

"Yes, that would suit me very well. Only you must dine

here, Mr. Wood. I will not hear of your going off to the Red Lion."

He hesitated, but she insisted. Considering the handsome allowance she was receiving from Mr. Wood's patron, she would be really ashamed to send him off to dine at the inn. Though she did wonder rather anxiously whether there was enough food in their female establishment to feed such a large man. They had killed a chicken, which was lucky; Martha could dress the giblets separately and send in the cold ham as well. And Judy had better go to the butcher for some collops of veal; she could call in at the Red Lion, cancel Mr. Wood's order, and bring back a bottle of claret. There was a gooseberry tart and half a pint of cream in the larder, and plenty of young green peas and strawberries in the garden. By the time she had worked out these plans and spoken to Martha in the kitchen, Mr. Wood had assembled the pieces of stick and canvas, and they trooped over to the common on the other side of the road, Diana and Nancy each in charge of a child and Mr. Wood in charge of the kite.

The common was a wild stretch of grass and brambles where the villagers grazed their beasts. The ground rose higher than the surrounding acres of green corn, so it was a good place to catch the wind. Mr. Wood had a little trouble in launching the canvas air toy, but he managed at last by throwing it up and running very hard. He ran remarkably well, Diana thought, for a man of forty-odd in hessian boots. The light, empty frame was caught in a spiral of air and carried upwards; once it was high enough to drift on the tide of the wind he played it with the skill of an angler holding a fish on his line.

Up and down the common they went, the children squealing with pleasure. Mr. Wood let Hop hold the string with him, so that he could feel the thrilling tug of the strange red and blue bird. Hop was transported with delight. What a good father this man must be, thought Diana.

"You have boys of your own, haven't you, Mr. Wood?"

"I have a son," he said, though in such a bleak manner that she was afraid she had been tactless. Then the kite was jerked away by another gust and he had to run with it.

Presently Diana felt she must return to the house to make sure Martha was not in difficulties over the dinner, and to get out her best dessert service, which had belonged to her mother. Leaving Nancy to look after the children, she slipped away. Martha was singing to herself in a cloud of steam, pleased to have company to cook for. Diana went upstairs to fetch the dessert plates, which were stored on the top of her wardrobe. She could not resist a glance out of her bedroom window. The kite-fliers were running at full tilt down the sloping ground towards the road, with the kite blowing ahead of them but losing height. At right angles to the running group a solitary horseman was trotting along the road: Mr. Roger Brownlees, probably on his way to Chelmsford.

He was riding a well-mannered bay mare who was perfectly broken to traffic, but the sight of a great scarlet and blue creature coming at her out of the sky was too much for her: she shied violently. Mr. Brownlees was not expecting this, he lost a stirrup and at the same moment the tail of the kite tipped the brim of his hat and flicked it off his head. He put up his hands instinctively, dropped the reins and lost his other stirrup, so that he was obliged to cling ignominiously round the mare's neck until she had stopped waltzing about in circles.

By the time this happened, the kite-flying party had reached the road, and they were all in fits of laughter.

"I do beg your pardon, my dear sir," Diana could hear Mr. Wood saying as he picked up his victim's hat and brushed off the dust with his sleeve. "I'm afraid we gave you a shocking fright."

"What the devil do you mean, sir, by playing the fool with that thing on the public highway?" demanded Mr. Brownlees angrily. "There might have been a serious accident. If the mare had bolted I might have been killed."

"Happily your prowess as a horseman preserved us from such a calamity," said Mr. Wood, tongue undoubtedly in cheek.

This made Mr. Brownlees angrier than ever. Poor man, he had nearly fallen off his horse in front of this impudent stranger, and his pride was wounded.

"If you think it diverting to play tricks on innocent users of the road, let me assure you the law takes a very different view. I am a magistrate—"

"I didn't mean to knock your hat off! It was the purest chance. In fact, I don't believe anyone could do it on purpose."

"Do it on purpose!" repeated Hop, standing close to his new friend.

Mr. Brownlees noticed Hop and Sukey for the first time.

"Those are Mrs. Pentland's children!"

He sounded as though he thought the kite-flying lunatic might also be a dangerous abductor. Diana decided it was time for her to intervene. She ran down the stairs and out of the house. By the time she reached them, both gentlemen were studying each other with unconcealed dislike. She had quite a struggle not to laugh.

"Good morning, Mr. Brownlees. May I introduce Mr. Wood to you? But I see you have already met."

Mr. Brownlees said in a slightly admonishing voice, "I did not know you were expecting a visitor."

"Well, after all, why should you?" asked Mr. Wood.

Soon after this Mr. Brownlees said stiffly that he must not keep Mrs. Pentland standing in the wind, and rode away.

Mr. Wood watched him go. "Is that gentleman the subject of your letter to Caversham?"

"Yes, he is," said Diana, rather defiantly.

Mr. Wood made no further comment.

When it was dinnertime he said he was as hungry as a hunter. She hoped she had got enough for him to eat. He could not change, of course, and had apologised for this. She put on a white muslin dress and her newest lace cap and joined him in the drawing room, where he was strolling about admiring the miniature of Oliver in his regimentals, the silhouette portraits of her parents and a black basalt urn filled with roses and sweet-smelling pinks from the garden.

"It is always a pleasure to me to see such a bouquet," he said unexpectedly. "Servants will jam flowers down like herrings in a barrel."

Diana was almost surprised into a direct question that would have sounded very ill-bred. He met her eye and answered it, unasked.

"I am a widower, Mrs. Pentland. Before you start to be sorry for me, I must tell you I have lived alone very comfortably for eleven years, apart from a few slight reservations about flower vases. I am not much used to domestic life."

Diana remembered how good he had been with the children and thought this a pity.

He turned his attention to the pianoforte. "I am glad you have such a good instrument. You asked Caversham if you might buy it—I don't know why."

"Well, the Noble Client will hardly expect his son to learn the pianoforte, and when it comes to spending his money on luxuries for myself and Sukey, I feel it is necessary to ask permission."

"The—what did you call him?"

"You were not meant to hear that," said Diana, blushing. "It slipped out."

"Why do you call him noble? Not on account of his character, I assume?"

"Hardly. A man who could betray a girl of sixteen and expose her to such desperate fear and misery—I found Eliza, you know—"

"You rescued her, from death perhaps. That young villain hadn't given her a thought." He stopped abruptly, perhaps feeling more compunction than Diana did about abusing their employer, though there was a hard, contemptuous expression in his very blue eyes. Not for him the subservience of Mr. Caversham towards his superiors.

After a brief pause, he said, "If that is how you view our client, why do you call him noble? Is that purely ironic?"

"Not entirely. He is a member of the nobility, isn't he?"

Mr. Wood looked at her very hard. "What makes you think so?"

However much he disliked Eliza's anonymous lover, thought Diana, the secret of Hop's paternity was to be preserved at all costs. He was now afraid that she had discovered some clue. It would be amusing to mislead him, but perhaps rather frivolous.

"We thought so from the day we first met. Because the evening before, when Eliza was driven back to Sloane Place, the carriage that brought her had a coronet on the door."

"Ah," said Mr. Wood, apparently satisfied.

He enjoyed his dinner and conversed agreeably on many topics. He had read widely and travelled, and he could talk about the war in Europe in a way Diana found invigorating after three years spent among people who seldom moved out of their own district. She kept thinking they ought to discuss her future plans but hardly wanted to begin.

At last he said abruptly, "Do you seriously consider marrying that fellow? I cannot understand it."

"You had him at a disadvantage. He did not show at his best."

"Good God, I hope not! If that was his best—you should remember, however, that these little upsets and *contretemps* are the very stuff of married life. That is where it differs so much from simply being in love. You deserve something better than Brownlees. He thinks too much of his own consequence and has no sense of humour. I don't advise you to accept him."

"You are mistaken, Mr. Wood," said Diana, her temper rising. "I am not asking for advice."

"Oh. Then what is it you want?"

"To be released from my promise, if I—when I remarry, so that I can tell my husband the truth about Hop's birth. I should not ask to give him the names of the parents even if I knew them—and you have taken very good care to see that I don't. All I wish is to share this secret with a man who must claim the right to share all my secrets."

There was a longish silence. Wood took a sip of wine and set down his glass.

Then he said, "I am sorry. I cannot release you from your promise."

"Then will you ask your client—"

"It would be useless. I am well aware of his opinion."

"But this is outrageous! You and Mr. Caversham, between you, have forced me into a position where I cannot marry again without either deceiving my husband or breaking my word to your—your precious client. And it is so utterly unreasonable. You are prejudiced against Mr. Brownlees, but you cannot pretend he is not a fit person to have charge of a young boy. He is kind, religious, respectable—"

"A little too respectable, perhaps. Has it not struck you that he may not be so anxious to play the part of Hop's stepfather if he learns the truth?"

"He certainly will not do so if he supposes I am the cast-off mistress of some wealthy libertine," she retorted bitterly, "and that is what he is bound to think when he finds out how I receive my income."

"Yes, I appreciate your difficulty. But my dear Mrs. Pentland, think of the alternative: your conduct has been irreproachable, yet in proving this you must disown Hop. What is he? The unwanted bastard child of unnamed parents. Their rank in society means nothing; it simply underlines the weakness, folly and self-indulgence of two people who ought to have known better. In my experience an upright country gentleman like Brownlees is the last person to condone the vices of the aristocracy. He might very well point out that Hop has no real claim on you, and that the man who has paid you to take care of him can afford to find another guardian."

"Nothing would induce me to part with Hop! There isn't a man in the world I would marry on those terms."

Mr. Wood smiled. "I thought you would say that."

"Yes, but you may be maligning poor Mr. Brownlees. I must say I had not considered the question properly, but I have no reason to believe. . . ."

Her voice trailed off uncertainly. She did not really know what Roger Brownlees' attitude would be. Because Wood had practically forbidden the banns, she had found herself talking as though there was a definite engagement. Actually her mind was in a turmoil. He observed her confusion.

"By the time you like a man well enough to marry," he said gently, "you will already have discovered that he is someone who can regard Hop as you do, a child who is now inseparably part of your own family. When that happens, I think I can make the Noble Client see reason.

Brownlees may be your man, though I doubt it. You have been acquainted for several years, yet I gather you never thought of marrying him until four days ago. I beg you, don't be in too much of a hurry."

They went back into the little drawing room and she rang for the tea tray almost immediately. Mr. Wood drank one cup before walking down to the Red Lion to pick up his chaise and drive back to town.

When they parted, he said, "I hope I haven't offended you by my abominable habit of plain speaking. I cannot tell you how much I admire your courage and spirit, and the happiness of the home you have made for both your children. I am sure you must sometimes be lonely. It would be tragic if you drifted into an unwise marriage on that account. Perhaps in the autumn we should consider your removing to another neighbourhood. Somewhere you might meet with rather more society."

After he had gone she sat alone in the darkening room, without lighting the lamp. Later she went to bed and lay awake, hearing the wind rattle the windowpanes. The day's events had disturbed her, and she felt she had been behaving lately with the silly impulsiveness of a school-girl. Although Brownlees' proposal had taken her completely by surprise, she had soon welcomed the idea as something possible and desirable. Until this morning and the incident of the kite. Of course he had made himself a little ridiculous, but what of it? Oliver had been very silly once or twice, after he had been drinking in the mess, and that had never worried her. If Brownlees was a man she could seriously contemplate marrying, surely she should not have been led into laughing at him behind his back.

What was she to do? She did not want to make the terrible mistake of marrying a man with whom she could not be happy. But neither did she want to make the more negative mistake of refusing a good offer because Mr. Wood said she would not be happy. Confound Mr. Wood

—what right had he to say that Brownlees would reject Hop if he knew the truth? And suppose she did refuse him; could she go on living at Palfreys, or would she find that her Eden had been spoilt for her? Wood had suggested she should remove to a new neighbourhood, which would mean uprooting the children and starting again among strangers. That might be yet another mistake.

What I want, thought Diana, is not a house-move in the autumn, but a change of scene now, as soon as possible, before Brownlees's sister gets here and starts quizzing me. Only where could I go?

She sat up in bed, punching her pillows to make them more comfortable. Last year she had taken the children to Southend, which they had all enjoyed; however, the strong air had not suited Sukey; it was too bracing. And the Miss Ficklings had gone with her, two sisters who lived in the village. They would not be free this summer, for they were going on a tour of the Lakes, and Diana did not think she would care for Southend without them.

I want some quiet, pretty retreat inland, not a smart watering place, she decided. I wonder if the Jacksons could suggest anything.

Mr. Jackson was the rector of the parish and his wife was a niece of Mrs. Caversham. It was through them that Palfreys had originally been rented for Diana. The lawyers had been anxious to settle her in a village where she could be sure of some pleasant neighbours to befriend and vouch for her. The Jacksons had not been let into the great secret; they simply knew Diana as a widow with two children who happened to be one of Mr. Caversham's many clients. There was not the smallest need for her to mention Mr. Wood's visit or the complications about Hop. She would simply say she needed a change of air, drop a hint about Mr. Brownlees and her own state of indecision, and Kitty Jackson would see her point exactly.

PART THREE

Brandham Castle

I

"Gig!" chanted Hop, his nose pressed against the window of the post-chaise.

At the same instant Sukey called out "Beehive!"

They were playing travelling picquet, a splendid game for a journey: the players scored points for various animals, objects and people seen on the way. Hop already knew the name of everything that went on wheels, though he could not always pronounce it. Sukey caught sight of a man with a wooden leg and asked how many points she could score for him.

Hop was so anxious to see the wooden leg that he scrambled across to the other side of the chaise.

"We'll all have wooden legs, Master Hop, if you kick us so," said Nancy placidly.

Nancy was a fairly calm traveller, which was just as well, for the children were not.

It now seemed a very long way from Great Wickfield in

East Anglia to Brandham in the Midlands. They had been
on the road since eight and would reach their destination
about seven, having changed into a different chaise with
fresh horses at five successive posting-inns. (They had
nearly left Sukey's doll behind in the change at Ayles-
bury, a calamity too terrible to contemplate.)

They were going to Brandham on the suggestion of
the Jacksons, who had been just as helpful as Diana
hoped. Kitty Jackson's brother Richard Turner had formerly run a school, a very good school, which had failed
inevitably, his sister said, though without explaining why.
He had been lucky in obtaining a new situation, through
family influence, as librarian at Brandham Castle. The
Turners had been given a house inside the grounds, actually built within the shell of the castle itself, and Kitty was
sure her sister-in-law would be delighted to have visitors.
She was finding Brandham rather quiet after Hampstead.

So letters had been exchanged and the whole business
arranged in less than a fortnight. Poor Roger Brownlees
had been going about with a hangdog expression; he
seemed to imagine he had a rival in Mr. Wood, which annoyed Diana for reasons she did not care to examine.
Well then, who was the fellow, he demanded. What had
he come for? And so forth. Diana was thankful to get
away.

She was glad for another reason. On the morning of
Mr. Wood's visit she had received a letter from some old
friends of army days. Tom Robinson had been seriously
wounded in Spain; he was recovering very slowly in the
noise and heat of London. Diana could not have invited
the Robinsons to stay with her at Palfreys; there wasn't
room. But as she was going away herself she offered them
the use of her house, garden, and servants for the month
she was to spend at Brandham. They had been embar-
rassingly grateful.

It was suddenly much quieter in the carriage; Hop had

dropped off to sleep in Nancy's lap. Sukey was yawning too. They were driving through a green countryside, much prettier, more wooded and varied than the country Diana had grown used to in Essex. The road was dipping towards a bridge. There was a confused skyline of buildings beyond: houses and a church. On their left a plantation of trees obscured the view, but as soon as this was passed they had a marvellous prospect of the river, and above the river rose two massive round towers joined by a great curving wall, perhaps forty feet high. The castle seemed to be poised in midair; it was encircled by trees and perfectly reflected in the still water below.

Diana caught her breath.

"Look, Nancy. That's where we're going."

"In there, ma'am? Us? Why, it's a sort of place for the King to live in!"

"Don't be alarmed. We are not visiting the owner, you know—merely a gentleman who is employed there, the brother-in-law of our rector at home. In fact, I never heard the owner's name."

A few minutes took them over the bridge and into the cobbled streets of a small market town. One of the postilions asked the way into the castle. They were directed up a short hill, through an archway and across another bridge—it must have been a drawbridge once, though it was now solid stone—spanning an artificial moat. The moat was covered with bright green weed and waterlilies. The carriage passed between some romantic-looking cavities of broken masonry, through a second archway and into a great enclosed court. There were high towers at each corner, and at the far end a grim, squarish building which looked extremely old. But on the right of the quadrangle, built into the actual fabric of the Castle and looking quite modest by comparison, was a fine Jacobean house with a facade of decorated stonework and long windows. On the opposite side, tucked under the furthest tower, were two smaller, plainer houses of the same period, and out of one of these there now came a thin man in black, smiling and waving his arms, to indicate where the carriage was to stop.

"Mrs. Pentland? Welcome to Brandham! How weary you must be after such a long journey. Your little lad is fast asleep, I see. Come in, come in: here is my wife, and the servants will attend to your baggage."

They went into the house. The children were carried straight upstairs and put to bed without too much washing. Sukey ate a bowl of bread and milk; Hop hardly woke for long enough to swallow a spoonful. After she had kissed them good night, and seen that Nancy was being taken care of by a friendly housemaid, Diana went into her own bedroom to wash her hands and face and comb her hair, before going down to make the acquaintance of her hostess, who up to now was hardly more than a shadow in a dark hall.

She already knew that Mrs. Turner was thirty-nine, two years older than her husband, and had two sons by a previous marriage: one now studying medicine in Edinburgh and the other a midshipman at sea. She was inclined to mother her clever, unworldly husband and managed to look larger than he did, without being taller.

Diana had brought the Turners letters from their relations, and the first ten minutes were taken up with delivering messages and describing how much the Jackson children had grown in the past year.

Diana had dined on the journey, but was glad to hear that tea would soon be brought in. She glanced about her. The Turners' drawing room was long and low, running through the whole house from front to back, with a window at either end. The front one gave on to the great central court of the castle, where the coach had set them down.

"May I go and look at the view from your other window?"

"By all means. I dare say it will surprise you."

The contrast was complete. Instead of enclosing stone there was a wide panorama. The grassy slopes below the window had been laid out as a pleasure-garden running down to the perimeter wall, and beyond, on the far side of the river, lay a land of woods and fields and distant hills, a serene pastoral with hardly a house in sight.

"What a charming scene!" she exclaimed, "and what a wonderful old place this castle is. I long to explore."

"If you are interested, I shall be delighted to show you round," said Mr. Turner eagerly. "Brandham is one of the oldest inhabited dwellings in the kingdom—we share the distinction with Berkeley, Raby and Warwick."

"In other words, the owners of all these properties have built themselves very comfortable houses inside their fortifications," remarked Mrs. Turner, who had taken a piece of netting and was working away industriously. "You must not imagine the Lamberts have been living all these centuries in a Norman keep, Mrs. Pentland. No doubt you notified the fine house opposite as you drove in. That is where the family lives now."

"And those impressive towers—are they quite deserted?"

"They were until recently," said Dick Turner. "But since he came of age three years ago, Mr. Lambert has been restoring one of them to a state of Gothic glory. Well, not precisely Gothic," he added thoughtfully. "I sometimes feel Mr. Lambert's taste for improvement has a little outrun the laws of probability—though I suppose it is actually possible that a returning crusader might have embellished his castle with Moorish mosaics."

"Mr. Lambert is the present owner of the Castle?"

"Oh no, my dear ma'am," Mrs. Turner informed her.

"Brandham Castle is the principal seat of Viscount Grove. I thought you must have known."

This was the sort of thing Diana never did know, but she accepted the rebuff meekly, and asked, "In that case, who is Mr. Lambert?"

"The Honourable Henry Lambert is the only son and heir of the present Viscount. An excellent young man, is he not, Richard? Well conducted, charitable, everything he should be."

"He seems a very fortunate young man," said Diana, "if he is allowed to improve his family home while his father is still alive. What does Lord Grove think about the Moorish mosaics?"

"Lord Grove has not lived at Brandham for many years. He has another estate in Hampshire and a house in London. His lordship is an intimate friend of the Prince of Wales—the Prince Regent, as I suppose one must call him, though considering it was his own unbridled depravity that drove his poor father mad, I wonder he dared to accept the title."

Mrs. Turner's dogmatic manner had the effect of making Diana want to take the opposite point of view, but on this subject one was forced to agree with her. The Regent and his friends really were beyond the pale.

Tea was brought in, and soon Diana was able to make her excuses and go to bed. She was very tired.

At breakfast next morning she assured her hostess that they were all thoroughly rested after their journey.

"Hop has been awake since six. I do hope he did not disturb the whole house."

"No, not at all. These walls are very thick. I trust your nurse has everything she needs for the children?"

"Yes, indeed. You have been so kind. I told Nancy to bring them down here, ma'am, as soon as they are ready to go out."

Mrs. Turner expressed her approval. Her husband had already gone over to the library, but was hoping to show Mrs. Pentland round the castle later in the morning.

Presently Nancy arrived with the children. Diana was proud of them; they looked so lively and fresh and good-tempered at this early hour, Sukey in her printed cotton dress and Hop all in red, which suited his dark hair.

Sukey came forward first, and Mrs. Turner exclaimed, "So this is Susannah! You are very like your Mama, my dear."

Sukey had inherited Diana's vivid colouring—golden brown hair and dark blue eyes; she had Oliver's snub nose and engaging if not beautiful features.

"And this is your brother. Well, he is a fine little fellow, though not at all—oh!"

The exclamation was so sudden that Diana looked round enquiringly at Mrs. Turner. Hop, for reasons of his own, had decided to present her with one of his toy soldiers. He was holding it out in his left hand, and she had caught sight of the deformed little finger. Diana was annoyed. Sentimental women were apt to make such an absurd fuss over this minor defect when they noticed it, saying things in front of the child which might be harmful once he was old enough to understand them and to feel himself some kind of freak.

Mrs. Turner, to do her justice, did not mention the finger. She merely said, in a voice which sounded slightly accusing, "He is not at all like you."

"He takes after his father's family."

Diana had first made this ambiguous reply when they went to live in Essex. Now she made it automatically. Most of the time she almost forgot that Hop was not her own son.

Mrs. Turner had asked to see the children but did not have much to say now they were here. She sat studying them, or at least studying Hop, until Diana suggested that Nancy should now take them out into the castle grounds. This had been talked of last night.

"This morning? Oh no, that will not do—that is to say, I do not think it will be convenient."

Nancy and the children were disappointed, and Diana felt rather put out. She was wondering how to protest without appearing rude, when one of the maids came in with a tale of some domestic crisis, and Mrs. Turner was obliged to hurry off to the kitchen.

Diana said to Nancy, "I don't know why you may not go into the garden, but I suppose it is not always convenient; probably the Turners have to ask permission of the gentleman who lives in the big house, Mr. Lambert. Perhaps you had better take a walk in the town instead."

Nancy and Sukey were enchanted by the idea of walking about the town to stare at people and shops. This was something much more novel than a garden. Hop was pleased too, when told there were sure to be horses and carts. They set off in high glee.

Mrs. Turner soon came back and asked where they had gone.

"I told Nancy to take them down into the town, ma'am. They need the air and exercise—"

"Into the town? Good heavens, why did you do that?"

"Because you said it was not possible for them to play in the grounds. Surely there is no reason why they should not visit the town? There is no infectious illness in Brandham?"

"No, certainly not. It was only—well, never mind; it cannot be helped and I dare say it won't signify."

What an odd woman she is, thought Diana. She wished the Jacksons had given her some warning of their sister-in-law's peculiarities.

Half an hour later Dick Turner came to take Diana on a tour of the older parts of the Castle. He was an admirable guide and his passion for his subject was infectious. He explained the original purpose of all the different ruins, and gave her a lively history of the former owners, medieval barons who spent most of their time at the wars, and who married wives called Blanche or Eleanor or Ursula—pretty and outlandish they sounded to Diana, who was used to names taken from either the Bible or from classical antiquity.

Presently they reached the southwest tower, where young Mr. Lambert had been making his improvements, and were suddenly transported into a world of exotic romance. The circular chamber on the ground floor contained a marble fountain which cast a perpetual spray of water against a wall of dark green tiles. The water ran down the tiles in a soft and shimmering veil that was cooling and delightful on a hot June day, though perhaps it was not the ideal effect for the English climate. The spiral staircase was carpeted in scarlet and the wall was lined with mosaics. The second chamber was hung with painted leather and there was a collection of small ivory and enamel objects in a cedar cabinet. The chamber at the top of the tower had walls entirely covered by a plaster frieze of heraldic devices and strange beasts, attenuated ladies in pavilions, knights on horseback, ships, dragons, and rustic merrymakers, all existing apparently in a precipitous world of mountain crags and deep ravines. The dark blue ceiling was painted with stars to imitate the sky at night. Diana felt the whole place was part of some unrecorded legend.

"Mr. Lambert must be an original," she suggested.

Dick Turner smiled. "He does not go around dressed as a Saracen or a troubadour. He is an elegant, clever young man who occupies his proper place in society. What you see here is the result of a romantic imagination without much critical check on it. Lord and Lady Grove separated when their son was twelve; his lordship lives at

Paraden, their great house in Hampshire; her ladyship brought up the children at Brandham. As virtual master of this ancient castle, young Henry has been able to indulge his fancy. His mother never found fault with his taste, and she is now dead. As yet he has no wife to please. But for the war, of course, he would have had the benefit of a Grand Tour."

They had now reached the second floor on their way down. Glancing through the narrow window, Mr. Turner said, "You can take a look at Mr. Lambert, ma'am. He is just crossing the court with his friend Lord Ledbury."

Diana looked out at the two young men. "Which is Mr. Lambert?"

"The one on the left. Very handsome, is he not?"

"Oh yes, certainly."

Henry Lambert was tall and slim. He was quietly dressed and wore no hat; a lock of his dark hair fell romantically across his well-shaped brow. His features were very good, his face a narrow oval, the chin pointed. Diana had never seen him before, yet she knew that face almost as well as her own. He was the exact image of what Hop might be in twenty years time.

It's not possible, she thought wildly. I must be going mad. Yet the likeness was unmistakable. He was passing in front of the window and she could observe him clearly. She had never seen such a strong resemblance between two people except in the case of twins. Here, she felt reluctantly convinced, was Hop's father, the Noble Client in person.

Incredulity was succeeded by panic. She wanted to run away and hide. This was absurd. Henry Lambert would not recognise her even if she walked straight up to him. He knew her name, but it was highly unlikely that she would be introduced to him while she was staying with his librarian. In any case, what did it matter? By some extraordinary chance she had discovered his identity, but he had nothing to fear from her, so what could she fear from him? The last thing either of them wanted, presumably, was to disturb their present arrangement.

All this time Mr. Turner had been leading her down the spiral stairs and promising a peep into the picture gallery to end their tour of the castle. He had Mr. Lambert's permission to take his visitors into the house.

Diana would have shied away from this, only she had seen Henry Lambert and his friend heading in the opposite direction. As it was, she hardly felt able to look intelligently at fine paintings and fine furniture, though she did ask, as they walked through the gallery, whether there were any modern portraits.

"No," said Dick Turner. "They are in the private apartments. The wall space in here was quite filled up by the present Lord Grove's father, who was a notable collector. There he is—painted by Alan Ramsay in 1766."

The sixth Viscount Grove wore the wig, the brocaded coat and ruffles of fifty years ago, which looked so strange today, yet the masterly painter had given him a face that remained alive and contemporary. His likeness to his grandson Henry Lambert was reasonable but not overwhelming. You could say that Hop might be descended from this man, not that he must be. Except for one thing they had in common. Diana had not been close enough to see Henry Lambert's left hand, but his grandfather's was clearly visible in the portrait. The hand of an aristocrat, untouched by toil and gracefully poised, with one joint missing from the little finger.

II

Diana retired to her bedroom and tried to work out how she had got herself into this extraordinary situation. Of all the places in England she might have visited, to find herself in the home of Hop's real father and his ancestors—it was too great a coincidence to be borne. Diana did not believe in coincidence. It always annoyed her when reading a novel that no heroine could ever see a mysterious lady in a churchyard, or be rescued from pirates by a passing stranger, without discovering that the lady was her long-lost mother and the rescuer her long-lost brother. Now something like this was happening to her and Hop, and it was not romantic but embarrassing.

After some minutes of brooding, she realised that there had been no great coincidence after all, merely a logical sequence of probabilities. The key to the mystery was Mr. Caversham. Kitty Jackson was Mrs. Caversham's niece, and it was on this account that the house in Great Wickfield had originally been rented. Dick Turner was Mrs. Caversham's nephew, he had obtained his post as librarian at Brandham through family interest, which meant no doubt, the influence of Uncle Caversham, the successful attorney who handled all the business of the Grove estates. It had obviously not struck Mr. Caversham that Kitty might innocently act as a link between her neighbour in Essex and her brother in Brandham, thus bringing Diana face to face with the Noble Client.

Diana now remembered rather guiltily that she had promised the lawyers not to move without first telling them where she wanted to go. But I never realised that applied to holidays, she excused herself. And anyway, if Mr. Wood hadn't come interfering and being so disagreeable about poor Brownlees I should never have come here at all. It's his fault, and I shall tell him so.

The nursery party came in to say how much they had enjoyed their walk in the town. There were some very nice shops, according to Nancy and they had also had the luck to be standing on the pavement outside the Lambert Arms when the York stagecoach stopped to change horses.

"The man said 'Horses On!' " Hop shouted, as he drove an imaginary coach and four between the bed and the dressing table. "Horses on!"

"Several ladies admired Master Hop," said Nancy complacently. "They seemed to know we was staying at the castle."

"I'm not pretty like Hop, am I, Mama?" said Sukey rather wistfully.

Diana reassured her. "He is still very little, and people like to admire little children and babies. They would not praise a big girl like you in case it made you vain."

Sukey seemed satisfied. Did she but know it, any attention Hop had attracted this morning came from a kind of impertinent curiosity she would never incur. The people here recognised his Lambert looks and wondered who he could be. And of course Mrs. Turner's odd behaviour at breakfast was now explained. It was very awkward, thought Diana, but she would simply have to brazen it out.

Mrs. Turner spent the afternoon trying to disentangle Hop's ancestry without appearing to do so. Diana was surprised that she did not ask a direct question, until she realised that Letitia Turner's blunt manner really covered a perpetual nervous uncertainty. She did not know whether her guests were slightly disreputable or unexpectedly distinguished, so she was not sure how to behave towards them.

Diana managed to stave off her curiosity without being either untruthful or discourteous. In return she found out one thing she herself wanted to know: Henry Lambert was an only son, and though he had three boy cousins they were still at school. So he must be Hop's father, not that she had seriously doubted this. When Eliza had first seen her baby, she had said he was the image of Henry. Later she had said that Henry was to be his name. When she went to see her lover, he had sent her back to Sloane Place in a carriage with a coronet on the door. Henry Lambert was the heir to a peerage; he was the same age, Diana calculated, as Eliza's brother, and if he had to make arrangements for the future of an illegitimate child his most likely agent would be Mr. Caversham, the family attorney.

The next two days passed quietly. Some ladies and gentlemen arrived to visit Mr. Lambert but Diana did not see them. She had found that it was quite easy to get out of the Castle grounds simply by crossing a footbridge over the moat, and she spent most of her time in the woods with the children and Nancy. On Sunday, having made sure that Henry Lambert and his household attended the chapel in the Castle, she took Sukey to the morning service at the parish church.

On Monday she set out alone to do a little shopping. Brandham was a small provincial town with no great pretensions, but to Diana, who lived all the year round in the depths of the country, the shops were very inviting, especially a superior one called Simpson's at the corner of Castle Street.

Having chosen some braid for a coat and matched up several skeins of embroidery silk, she lingered to examine the materials on display. Really, these muslins were very pretty and astonishingly cheap, with every variety of sprig and spot and stripe. The coloured nankeens and cottons, too. It might be a good idea to lay in a stock while she was here, both for herself and the children.

Some more people came in and she was aware that the waiting shopkeeper wanted to serve them.

"Don't let me keep you," she said. "I shan't buy anything more. I just want to see what you have, and I shall come back another day and make my choice."

The man murmured his thanks and hurried off. While she was still fingering snowy folds of muslin, she caught snatches of fussy obsequiousness going on behind her.

"This way, if you please, ma'am. This way, sir. . . . A chair for Mrs. Webb, Sally. . . . Are you quite comfortable, ma'am?"

The shop people seemed so anxious to please that Diana wondered whether Henry Lambert himself was among the customers. She took a quick look. There were only two of them: a lady in a smart bonnet, now seated at the counter, and a pale, plain young man with ginger hair and the expression, Diana decided, of a discontented camel.

"Please show me some gloves, Mr. Simpson," the lady was saying languidly. "My maid has forgotten to pack a single pair, and my husband refuses to be seen with me until I am decently gloved."

"There is no need to talk such affected nonsense, Eliza," said the man with the camel sneer. "It's nothing to me what sort of a wild figure you cut down here in the country, but I suppose you don't want your hands and arms burnt black by the sun. That would not please you at all."

The shopkeeper, wisely ignoring the matrimonial bickering, began to lay out his wares.

Diana, struck by a name and a voice, looked round again, and this time the lady had moved and it was possible to see her properly. She was unusually tall and looked much too thin. Could this haggard, fashionably dressed young woman be the plump girl who had wandered into Sloane Place three and a half years ago and in such dire need?

Diana was still gazing at her uncertainly when their eyes met and she had her answer. Eliza recognised her instantly. She gasped and clutched the edge of the counter.

"My wife is not well," exclaimed the young man, stepping closer to support her.

There was an immediate stir. Somebody untied her bonnet strings, somebody else was sent for a glass of water and a vinaigrette, and Mr. Simpson said that doubtless Mrs. Webb had been overcome by the heat of the day.

While this was going on Diana quietly left the shop.

III

======

Diana walked back to the Castle, feeling very disturbed.
To find both Hop's parents in Brandham was something
she would never have expected. What were they doing
here? Well, what do you think they are doing, asked a
cynical spectator inside her head. Exactly what they were
doing four years ago? Judging from Eliza's style of dress
and the fawning behaviour of the shop people, she was
almost certainly one of the grand guests at the Castle.
Only she was now married to that cross-looking man and
her name was Mrs. Webb, while Henry Lambert was not
married at all. So he could have married the poor girl
when the baby was born, thought Diana. Too selfish, I
suppose, or perhaps she wasn't rich enough.

She crossed the bridge over the moat and turned aside
on to the grass, thinking she would stay out here and
compose herself before returning to the librarian's house.

A man came out of a small ruined turret at the end of the bridge, as though he had been lying in wait for her.

"Mrs. Pentland! I should like a word with you, if you please."

Diana stopped, her heart thumping. "Yes, Mr. Lambert?"

"May I ask what you are doing in Brandham?"

She had intended, if he challenged her, to apologise for bringing Hop to the Castle, explaining how it had happened. At the moment she was feeling too angry and disgusted with Henry Lambert to explain anything, so she said coldly, "I am staying with Mr. and Mrs. Turner."

"You know very well what I am asking. What is your ulterior motive?"

Diana did not answer. She was struck dumb by the extreme oddness of disliking a person who reminded her so strongly of her darling Hop. In a sort of trance she saw the lopped-off finger on his left hand.

"Are you after money?" enquired Henry Lambert disagreeably. "Or have you simply come to make trouble?"

"Of course I don't want anything of the sort."

"Perhaps you were hoping to thrust yourself and your children into our family circle? Let me tell you, ma'am, you have miscalculated. Now that my mother is dead, I am indifferent to any scandal you could provoke here, and as for Lord Grove, he never comes to Brandham and our paths seldom cross. I advise you to go and look for him elsewhere."

"I haven't the faintest desire to thrust myself into your exalted family!" retorted Diana. "And Lord Grove is the last person I want to meet!"

Henry laughed. "What a pity you found that out too late."

And with this incomprehensible parting shot he walked away, leaving her almost literally speechless with rage. Not only rage but fear, after a moment's reflection, for she had burnt her boats by quarrelling with the Noble Client, who apparently thought that because he paid for her keep he could treat her like some inferior menial. Now perhaps he would cut off supplies to punish her. Or much worse, try to take Hop out of her care. What was she to do? If only I had someone to advise me, she thought. And immediately the comforting image of Mr. Wood took shape in her mind's eye. She would write to him today. She ought to have written before, as soon as she found herself in this scrape, only she had been annoyed by his autocratic way of telling her not to marry Roger Brownlees, and she wished to retain her independence. Now she would be thankful for an arm to lean on.

The morning was hot, the midday sun carved short shadows round the great grey slabs of tower and wall. Diana was exhausted by the shocks of the last hour. The hall of the librarian's house was pleasantly cool, and she was hoping to creep upstairs unseen when Mrs. Turner called to her from the drawing room.

She was obliged to go in there, and found that Mrs. Turner had callers: Mrs. Smith, the wife of the castle chaplain, who occupied the house next to the Turners, and two Brandham ladies, Mrs. Gill and Mrs. Redmayne. They all said they were delighted to make the acquaintance of Mrs. Pentland and took her apart with their hopeful, inquisitive glances.

"And are we not to have the pleasure of seeing your interesting children?" asked Mrs. Gill.

"I am afraid they are not available, ma'am. They are out in the woods with their nurse."

"In the woods?" Mrs. Gill tittered. "Are you a disciple of Rousseau, my dear ma'am?"

Mrs. Redmayne had a topic of even greater interest. "I heard that Mrs. Webb is in a delicate situation."

This created a mild sensation, not least with Diana, though she was careful to hide her interest.

"I have heard nothing," said Mrs. Smith in an injured voice. "And I should certainly have thought, considering my husband's position—"

"She fainted in Simpson's this morning. I was in there ten minutes later and Sally Simpson told me. Of course they said it was the hot weather, but she's been married two years and it's high time she started her nursery."

This unleashed a babble of vague speculation, and Diana, anxious to learn more about Eliza, felt there was no harm in saying that she thought she had seen Mrs. Webb in the shop.

"Is she a very tall young lady?"

"Yes, unusually so," said Mrs. Redmayne. "She used to be rather plump as a girl and I think it suited her better. Now she lives in London she has become far too thin."

"Did she grow up in Brandham?"

"Of course," said Mrs. Redmayne, surprised. "Here in the Castle, with her mother and brother. She was formerly the Honourable Elizabeth Lambert."

It was Diana's third shock of the morning, and it left her in a state of confusion with every accepted idea having to be thought out again. Sitting silent while the other women gossiped, she tried to make sense of it all.

Henry and Eliza were not lovers; they were brother and sister. Hop had inherited his looks, not from his father but from his uncle. It was only in stories that children were exactly like their parents; in real life, features more often passed at one remove, from a grandparent, uncle or aunt. Why did I never think of that?, Diana wondered. Eliza looked at her newborn son and wept because he reminded her of her beloved brother—the brother she dared not tell about the baby because he would hate her for being so wicked. And now Diana was seized with a terrible doubt: had she given Eliza away?

The guests got up to leave.

When they had gone, Mrs. Turner said sourly, "I never had so many morning callers on one day since we arrived in Brandham. They all came to quiz you. I suppose you know that."

Diana hardly took this in. She was too preoccupied in trying to remember what she had said to Henry Lambert during that acrimonious interview which had begun to puzzle her very much indeed.

She had taken it for granted that he was Eliza's lover, Hop's father, the man whom she had always called the Noble Client—justly annoyed at her turning up on his doorstep, though showing his annoyance in a way that was quite unreasonable. But this was not so. The real father must be another of Caversham's clients—nothing strange in this, a superior attorney like Caversham might handle the affairs of a dozen great families.

But in that case, where did Henry Lambert come in? He had obviously heard about Hop. Perhaps he had actually seen him in the Castle grounds, but who did he suppose the Pentlands were? Could he be in the secret after all? Perhaps the older, more worldly Eliza had found the courage to confide in her brother. Diana tried to remember exactly what he had said.

"Now that my mother is dead, I am indifferent to any scandal you could provoke here."

That did not sound like a brother protecting his sister's reputation. And there were those references to Lord Grove, which had seemed irrelevant even at the time. . . . Light dawned suddenly, and with it a wave of incredulous wrath.

Henry Lambert thought she was his father's mistress.

The mistress of an elderly rake who probably painted his face and wore corsets like his friend the Regent. She was supposed to have sold herself to this repulsive old satyr, and then, presumably abandoned by him to have come up here hoping to indulge her greed and spite, and prepared to use Grove's bastard as a trump card.

It was such an outrage to everything she felt and believed and held dear that for a moment—only for a moment—she almost wished she had not adopted Hop. But nothing would make her regret that, however cruelly she was misjudged.

And she was going to be misjudged, she realised; there was nothing she could do about that. It was part of the bargain she had struck with Caversham and Wood, when she accepted the Noble Client's very handsome allowance, and in any case her compassion for another woman would have ensured her silence. She could never betray Eliza.

IV

Several hours later, when she went upstairs to change for dinner, Diana found a slip of paper folded small and tucked into the frame of the looking-glass on her dressing-table. She opened and read it.

I must speak to you. Please come to the southwest tower tomorrow at ten. E.W.

Eliza must be suffering the most acute anxiety ever since she caught sight of me in the shop, thought Diana. Perhaps she too thinks I have come here to make trouble, poor girl. And of course she is far more vulnerable to scandal than Hop's father would be.

Accordingly, next morning after breakfast Diana strolled as inconspicuously as possible towards the tower that Henry Lambert had decorated so fantastically. It was not easy to be inconspicuous in the great open court, overlooked by so many windows, but she loitered cautiously in the shadow of the keep and had a good look round before slipping into the arched doorway. The only creature to notice her was an old dog who lay panting in the heat. He was always about the place; she had heard one of the servants call him Bruno.

The room with the cooling fountain was empty; Diana ran up one carpeted twist of the spiral and saw a white figure standing by the cedar cabinet on the next floor.

"Mrs. Pentland! I was so afraid you would not come!"

"I'm afraid I must have caused you a great deal of apprehension," said Diana. "I am so sorry. I would never have visited Brandham if I had known it was your family home. When I first saw your brother—"

"Henry spoke to you, did he not? He has no idea of the truth—of what happened three years ago—but you did not tell him anything?"

"Nothing at all. . . . I promise you."

"I could not bear him to find out and despise me," said Eliza, her eyes filling with tears. "Though this is not why I wanted to see you. I am so anxious to hear about my baby, my little Henry. Is he a good boy? Is he strong and healthy? You don't know how I have longed for news of him."

She gazed imploringly at Diana. The contours of her face had a look of settled unhappiness and she was far too worn for her age—she could not be more than twenty even now.

Diana assured her that Henry was a dear little boy, affectionate and lively, had hardly known a day's illness and was the pet and darling of their small household. "Sukey—do you remember my Sukey? She is devoted to him."

"Oh, I am so glad! You cannot imagine—tell me more: has he learnt his letters?"

"Well, not yet. Three and a half is rather early, and I don't think it is good for children to be forced."

"Of course not. It was silly of me. I know so little about young children, no one would ever suppose that I was a mother! I was a very unnatural one; I am sure you thought I was dreadfully heartless, Mrs. Pentland, when I said I didn't want my baby—"

"Certainly not. You were under such a great oppression of spirits, and in any case it was hardly possible—"

"I was too young to know what I was losing. I let him go, and all for what? So that I could return home as though nothing had happened, come out and go to balls, like other girls. Only I wasn't like other girls and it was all a horrid sham. I married the first man who asked me, simply because I wanted another baby that I could keep, and God has punished me for that too. Horace and I fight all the time and I shall never have any more children."

"My dear Mrs. Webb, you must not give up hope so early. You have not been married so very long, and once you do have children I expect you and your husband will settle down very comfortably. The first years of marriage are often rather stormy, you know."

As she uttered these platitudes, Diana wondered whether they could have any application to Eliza, who stood there looking so wretched twisting her expensive parasol in her restless hands, and begging for anecdotes about the child she had given away so thankfully when he was a fortnight old.

"You will let me see him, won't you? Perhaps, now we have met again, he could sometimes pay me a visit?"

Diana was saved from answering this question by the sound of footsteps on the stair, and a man's voice calling, "Eliza! Are you up there?"

Eliza made a grimace. "It's Horace—my husband. I shall have to go."

Mr. Horace Webb appeared on the turn of the stair. "What are you doing in here? I have been hunting for you everywhere: everyone else is ready to start and the Desmonds are expected before eleven—"

"Who cares about the Desmonds?" said Eliza.

"Henry does, and you ought to, considering she is your

cousin and such a point is always made of your being brought up together. Do come along." All this time Horace Webb had been staring at Diana with the unthinking rudeness of the rich.

Eliza turned to her with a rather tremulous smile. "Goodbye, my dear ma'am. I hope you will enjoy the rest of your stay at Brandham. Perhaps we shall meet again." There was a note of entreaty here.

As the Webbs made their way downstairs, Diana could hear him saying, "What induced you to speak to that woman? Don't you know she is the one Henry was telling us about?"

She did not hear Eliza's reply. She remained a little while longer in the tower, feeling very sad. As far as Eliza was concerned, the adoption of her baby had been a tragedy.

Not a tragedy for Hop: he had a secure and happy home with every reasonable hope of a good life ahead of him. But the device of passing him off as Oliver's son, all the secrecy and pretending, with its tiresome consequences for Diana, had been intended to protect Eliza Lambert, to give a second chance to the life she had nearly ruined while still in the schoolroom. And what had she done with that chance? Married a man she didn't care for, because she was pining for the child she gave away.

Diana had just left the tower when a smart open barouche drawn by a team of grey horses came jingling through the gatehouse arch and stopped outside the Castle House. There were two gentlemen on the box and a lady with two small boys inside. These must be the Desmonds, who were expected before eleven by Henry and not very welcome to Eliza.

Everyone got down from the barouche except the driver, and at the same moment five or six people trooped out of the house, and there were greetings and laughter while they all stood on the steps. Diana stayed where she was, pretending to examine a fine piece of stone carving over a doorway and putting on a soulful expression. She had no intention of walking past Henry Lambert and his friends as though she wanted them to notice her—that accusation of thrusting herself in had badly stung her pride. She had seen Henry and his brother-in-law on the doorstep, though not Eliza.

Apparently they were all going on a party of pleasure, and there was some good-humoured argument about who should travel in the barouche and who in the carriages that were being brought round from the Castle stables.

The little boys, bored by the delay, began to wander away from their mother. The younger child, who was about the same age as Hop, came trotting past Diana with a purposeful glint in his eye. Idly glancing after him, she saw the old mastiff Bruno lying in a shady recess of the wall.

"Don't go too near the dog, my dear," she said.

The little boy paid no attention to the strange lady. His father suddenly grasped what was happening. Impotent on the box of the barouche, he shouted: "Charley! Don't touch him!"

Diana saw the white gleam of a bone between the dog's paws. He lifted his head with an ominous growl, just as she darted forward and snatched Charley out of harm's way.

Charley let out a howl of rage and terror. He was probably more frightened by Diana than the dog, for he punched her with his little fists, crying: "Bad lady! Bad lady! Put me down."

"I won't hurt you, my love. You're quite safe." Diana held firmly on to him in case Bruno was still prepared to bite. But Bruno picked up his bone and took himself off in a hurry at the sight of Charley's father advancing with the coach-whip in his hand.

The boy's mother arrived even before her husband.

"Charley, you silly little goose—my dear ma'am, how can I thank you? He might have been so dreadfully bitten. I do hope the dog didn't bite you instead. I saw him snap."

"No, I assure you—he never touched me."

"Thank God for that. Let me take Charley—he is very heavy, isn't he? No, she is not a bad lady, you scamp. She is a very good, kind, brave lady, and you had better say thank you to her at once."

"We really are uncommonly grateful to you, ma'am," said Charley's father.

Diana heard Henry Lambert saying, "If that dog is going to attack children I shall have to have him shot."

"Oh Henry, no!" said Mrs. Desmond. "Poor old Bruno. Any dog will snap if he thinks his bone is going to be taken. It was my fault, I should have been watching the boys instead of gossiping. Had it not been for Mrs. . . ." She paused, on a note of enquiry.

"Mrs. Pentland," interposed Henry. He added stiffly, "May I introduce my cousins to you, ma'am? Mr. and Mrs. Frank Desmond."

Diana could not help feeling a little sorry for Henry. Having made such a speech about not including her in his family circle, he was now obliged to present her to his cousins because she had saved their child from being savaged by his dog. This appealed to her sense of the absurd.

The Desmonds were a most attractive couple. He had the black hair, fine profile and cleft chin of so many Irishmen, and a great deal of Irish charm, though his voice and manner were completely English. She was a slim, quicksilver creature, not so much beautiful as giving an impression of beauty through her vivacity and sweetness.

They went on telling Diana how grateful they were, but she brushed aside their thanks and made her escape as soon as she could. She had no wish to impose on their gratitude.

As soon as she returned to the librarian's house, Mrs. Turner pounced on her. "Couldn't you have kept out of the way? Why did you have to let them all see you?"

Diana stopped sharp. "If you were watching you must have seen what happened. Do you think I should have left little Charley Desmond to his fate?"

"I don't suppose Bruno would have done more than growl. And it is so awkward for us—you do not seem to think or care—but Mr. Lambert has been asking all sorts of questions, and he is very angry. He wanted to know where you had come from and how Richard's sister came to know you, and when he heard that Mr. Caversham had introduced you to the Jacksons, he was angrier than ever. It is quite plain there is some sort of disgraceful connection between your children and the Lamberts—only please don't tell me what it is, for I don't want to know about such horrid things. Only I think you should have spared us the humiliation of being tarred with such a brush."

Diana was conscience-stricken. She had not considered that her hosts might be made to suffer as a result of Henry Lambert's ill-founded suspicions.

"I'll leave at once," she said impulsively. "At least, not quite at once, because I cannot go straight home. I have lent my house, you know, for another three weeks. But I will find somewhere to take the children, Mrs. Turner, and then you will not be troubled by Mr. Lambert's disapproval any more."

Mrs. Turner began to change her tune. She did not want—she had not meant—it was simply that she had to think of everything herself, Richard being too innocent to see when he was being threatened. She then tried to behave in a natural, friendly manner, going into a long recital of all she had heard about the Desmonds.

"She was Miss Maria Cosway, a niece of the late Lady Grove, and after her mother's death she spent a great deal of time at the Castle. Sir Charles Cosway was in the diplomatic service, I believe. Mr. Desmond belongs to a noble Irish family. His elder brother will come into a title and large estates over there, so a cousin on their English side left his property to Mr. Frank. Edenworth Hall, three miles outside Brandham: a beautiful old place—that is to say, I have never been inside, but you can see the house from the road. . . ."

Diana was quite interested, because she had taken a fancy to the Frank Desmonds, though she was really wondering all the time how soon she could get herself and the children away from Brandham, which now seemed desirable from every point of view.

V

"A lady spoke to me just now, ma'am," said Nancy, "when I stepped out for a breath of air. She asked me a lot of questions about Master Hop."

"What sort of a lady?" asked Diana, uncomfortably certain that she knew the answer.

"I think she is the sister of the gentleman who lives here: the one who is going to be a lord when his father dies. Is it true that you are connected with all these great people, ma'am?"

"I'm afraid not, Nancy. The lady did not tell you so, did she?"

"Oh, no, ma'am. It was the servants here who said that. On account of Master Hop's finger being different from other people's. That's nothing, I told them. It happens all the time. The miller's wife in Little Wickfield had a baby last year with six fingers on each hand. It was only when the lady began to take such an interest in him that I wondered."

"Mrs. Webb is very anxious to have a son of her own. She has no children yet, and it is inclined to weigh on her mind."

This satisfied Nancy for the time being, but for how long? Diana was feeling hunted. We must get away from here, she thought again.

She had been invited with the Turners to drink tea that evening at the Chaplain's House next door. She knew Mrs. Turner found her presence unwelcome and did not want to take her to be quizzed by the good ladies of Brandham, so she made the classic excuse. She had a shocking headache, was quite unfit for company.

After Mr. and Mrs. Turner had left for the tea-drinking, she sat alone in their rather prim drawing room, searching for a way out of her difficulties.

She could not go back to Great Wickfield yet. Mary Robinson had been so desperate and so grateful for a peaceful haven where Tom could recuperate; they had a niece with them, helping to nurse him, and there simply would not be room for the Pentlands as well.

If only she had written to Mr. Wood. Once again she had put off writing. It was hard to say why. He was such a sensible, practical person, and he also had the gift of making her feel that she was a charming and witty young woman and that her life and surroundings were exceptionally interesting and delightful. All this without the slightest touch of gallantry or improper familiarity. Perhaps this was the very reason why she could not bring herself to write. No man who had that effect on women was ever unaware of it. Mr. Wood might be over forty and not at all handsome, he might have no one but the servants to arrange the flowers in his widower's establishment, but that would not be for lack of volunteers. Diana did not wish to become one of those unattached females

who read too much into the professional kindness of cler-
gymen, doctors, or lawyers. If Mr. Wood himself ever
showed signs of wishing to extend their acquaintance, that
would be different. She stood gazing at the view from the
window. The evening light cast a radiance over the English countryside so that it seemed as unreal as a Claude
landscape. If only one could escape into such a beautiful
and serene world. . . .

She was brought back to the present by the arrival of a
visitor.

"Mrs. Desmond has called, to see you, ma'am," announced the Turners' maid.

"Oh. Please ask her to come in."

It was a pleasure to receive the pretty young woman
she had met that morning. Maria Desmond had now
changed into a dress of rose-coloured gauze and had been
dining at the castle. She had come to repeat her thanks to
Diana for rescuing Charley from the jaws of Bruno.

"You are very obliging, ma'am. I do hope Charley has
forgiven me for my shocking interference?"

"Hardly, I'm afraid. He cannot believe that any dog
would bite *him*. And Francis, our elder son, was quite
disappointed because there was no blood. What little ego-
tists boys are! I believe you have one of your own?"

"Yes, I have," said Diana, looking straight back at her
and annoyed to feel herself blushing.

"I must tell you, Mrs. Pentland, that I have a second
reason for calling on you. My cousin seems to have been
extremely uncivil to you yesterday; he now very much re-
grets this, and I have been sent over here as an emissary
to find out whether—well, in short, to beg your pardon."

Diana took a deep breath. "Is Mr. Lambert apologising
for what he thought, or merely for saying it?"

"Both, I think. There is a quite extraordinary likeness
running through that family, but it often skips a generation, as in the case of the present Viscount, and sometime

crops up in the female line, and we all told Henry that there is no reason why you or your husband should not have inherited a strain of Lambert blood even without knowing it."

"I could have told Mr. Lambert that myself, if he had given me the chance."

This was disingenuous. If he had given her the chance, Diana would have given away the whole truth, under the impression that he was the Noble Client. Still, she might as well make the most of Mrs. Desmond's suggestion.

"I am afraid my cousin is too impulsive. He is inclined to speak without reflecting; then he is sorry later. Do you want him to make you a formal apology? I am sure he will do so, if that is what you wish—"

"Good heavens, no! Do not suggest such a thing, Mrs. Desmond. I should be horribly embarrassed. Please tell Mr. Lambert that as far as I am concerned, the matter is closed."

"That is very forgiving of you," said Maria Desmond, smiling. She quickly changed the subject by asking how long Diana intended to stay at Brandham.

"I hope to leave as soon as I have made some other arrangements. It is a little awkward; we cannot go home because I have lent my own house to some friends."

"But surely there is no reason for you to hurry away?"

Diana was taken aback. Henry Lambert's animosity had at least provided her with a valid excuse for wanting to leave Brandham immediately. Now he had recanted, and she could not give her real reason. She muttered something about having upset Mrs. Turner.

Luckily this made sense.

"She is supposed to be rather difficult," said Maria. "They had a school that failed, chiefly because she managed to fall out with so many of the parents. Mr. Caversham warned my cousin of this when he was recommending Mr. Turner for the post of librarian. Henry says it doesn't matter whom she upsets here so long as she doesn't burn down the library. But I can imagine that you might not be altogether compatible. Do you know, I have just had the most delightful notion: you and your children must come to Edenworth and stay with us!"

"But I could not possibly do that, Mrs. Desmond!" exclaimed Diana, aghast. She was trying to run away from Eliza and she could hardly go to visit her cousins.

"Why not? We should so like to have you."

Maria was very persistent. She had taken a fancy to Diana—indeed it was mutual—and perhaps she was intrigued by the idea of the little boy, whose descent (so she thought) was part of some bygone mystery. Very well-born and extremely wealthy, she had the natural simplicity, the unpretentious manners that such people can afford if they choose.

Having tried in vain to refuse her pressing invitation, Diana said at last, "I think I must tell you one of the things Mr. Lambert accused me of: trying to thrust myself and my children into his family circle. We do not belong to the same rank in society, and I prefer to keep to my own station."

"Good heavens, how pompous Henry can be!" said Maria, disgusted. "There are times when one is quite ashamed of him. I can promise you, if you come to Edenworth, you will see only the kind of people you might meet in any country village. Frank and I are complete rustics. We never entertain our great neighbours and we are too occupied to waste time thinking about ranks in society or proper stations. And as for the Lambert family circle, you won't get into that, for they are not likely to visit us uninvited."

"Are you sure?"

Maria laughed like a little girl. "Henry is so busy with his improvements, he prefers to summon people to Brandham. And we are apt to humour him. It's less trouble than taking umbrage. As for his sister, she looks down on her country cousins these days."

So perhaps it would be safe to go to Edenworth Hall for a short stay. It would certainly be wiser than remaining at Brandham, Diana reflected.

PART FOUR

PART FOUR

Edenworth Hall

I

Mrs. *Turner was very much put out. Having made it clear* that she wanted to be rid of her disreputable guests, it was extremely annoying to have them spirited away to Edenworth by Mr. and Mrs. Desmond, who ought by rights to ignore a family of nobodies with such equivocal origins. Diana was aware of having treated the Turners shabbily. She had made use of them and then accepted a more flattering invitation. It was not at all the way she liked to behave, but she felt it absolutely necessary to leave Brandham Castle.

She was not really certain whether or not it would be a good thing for Eliza to see her son, whether it might bring her greater happiness or greater misery. Diana did not even think that she herself was the right person to take that decision. She was quite convinced that this was not the time or place. Eliza was still suffering from the shock of finding Hop again, she seemed to be in a highly nervous state, and any meeting she manoeuvred at Brandham was liable to have far too many spectators, including Henry Lambert and Horace Webb, the two people who must not be allowed to guess the truth.

Once I am back at home, thought Diana, I must explain to Mr. Caversham or Mr. Wood what has happened, and they can decide what is best.

On Thursday morning a chaise arrived to convey the Pentlands to Edenworth Hall, about three miles from Brandham by the turnpike road. It was a large brick house built during the previous century, with the usual pillared portico and rows of large windows letting plenty of light into high, well-proportioned rooms. An avenue of walnut trees led straight up to the house, and an old-fashioned parterre with a series of lawns and hedges sloped away towards the river at the back.

"Not an improvement to be seen," said Maria, cheerfully, as she welcomed Diana into a hall paved with black and white marble. "We are shockingly behind the times."

Diana thought the whole aspect of Edenworth delightful.

Sukey and Hop were very excited to be staying in a house with other children; they had never done this before, or seen anything like the suite of nurseries on the top floor, where there was space for a little boy with a hobby horse to gallop from one end to the other as though he was out of doors. Francis Desmond was a year younger than Sukey and Charley three months younger than Hop. There was also a baby girl, Henrietta, born at Easter.

"I think they will all get on very nicely," said Maria, after they had left the nursery party and she had taken Diana into the summer breakfast room where cold meat and fruit were laid out for luncheon.

"The children are making friends," agreed Diana, "though I'm afraid my poor little Nancy is very much in awe of your nurse."

"Then she's in good company," said Frank Desmond, laughing. "Maria is terrified of her. I am the only person in this house who can manage Nurse."

"Oh, we all know you can charm birds off any bush," said his wife in a teasing voice but throwing him a glance of unabashed love and admiration.

There was one other visitor, Captain Walter Desmond, an officer in Wellington's army who had brought home despatches from the Peninsular and been granted a few weeks' leave. He was an agreeable young man, on very close terms with his brother and sister-in-law.

"Your little Hop has quite won my heart," continued Maria, "and he is such a perfect Lambert! One can hardly wonder at the sensation you caused in Brandham. What a very strong strain that must be, to keep on reappearing. Is there really no one in either of your families who looks like him?"

From this innocent question Diana realised that Maria honestly believed her to be quite in the dark about the supposed connection. Feeling rather a fraud, she said truthfully that she had never seen anyone at all like Hop until she came to Brandham.

"But I gather that the Lamberts themselves do not all inherit the likeness," she said, with a certain amount of cunning. "Mrs. Webb does not resemble her brother."

"No, she takes after her father—not in her features, but her large build and fair colouring come from him. Lord Grove himself is the exception who proves the rule; both his father and his son were born with all the Lambert characteristics and he has none of them."

"According to Henry," remarked Frank, "his father is jealous of him on that account. He says that's one reason why Grove dislikes him so."

"I don't believe that Grove does dislike him," said Walter Desmond. "He simply ignores him. Of course we all know Henry detests his father."

"You cannot entirely blame him," said Maria. "Henry adored his mother and took her side, as a romantic boy might be expected to. And Grove did treat my poor aunt abominably."

Diana saw the Desmond brothers exchange a glance of unspoken comment, and recalled various details about Eliza's mother that she had picked up three years ago in Sloane Place. Poor Mama, her life had been so sad; she had become so besotted about her own health that she had failed to notice her sixteen-year-old daughter was about to have a baby.

"No one could pretend that Grove was a good husband," said Frank. "All the same I see what Walter means: Henry is unreasonable. It was agreed at the time of the separation that Lady Grove should live at Brandham, so of course her husband kept away, and after her death he let Henry go on living there undisturbed. So Henry goes round telling everyone that his father neglects the place and cares nothing for the family honours. Yet when Grove does interfere—when he tried to prevent Eliza marrying Horace Webb, for instance—Henry flew into a rage and called him a tyrant. How odd and inconsistent everybody is except ourselves! Mrs. Pentland, may I carve you another slice of ham?"

"What I could never understand," said Walter, passing Diana's plate, "is why Eliza wanted to marry Webb. Henry supported her because Webb is very clever and a friend of his: they are both interested in some Evangelical charity, I believe. Which is no reason for a girl like Eliza to choose him as a husband. She could have done better than Horace Webb."

Diana thought how odd it was that she, the stranger, was the one person in the room who could have given the true reason. Naturally she said nothing. She could not help being fascinated by this discussion of the Lambert family, and was rather sorry when Frank had a sudden onset of propriety and changed the subject.

Later in the afternoon a landaulet drawn by two pretty long-tailed ponies was brought to the front door, and Maria drove Diana round the park and through the village, pointing out all the local landmarks and apparently knowing the history of every cow, sheep or tree, let alone every cottage with all its inhabitants.

It was haymaking time, and next day the entire Desmond family, apart from the baby, went out to one of the meadows to watch the mowers at work. The Pentlands, of course, went, too, Sukey and Hop entranced by the treat of helping to toss and turn the drying grass. Sukey staggered along, clasping a great bundle of the stuff, scarlet in the face and with her sunbonnet over one ear. Hop and his new friend Charley pelted each other with soft green handfuls, rolled and tumbled among sweet-smelling hay billows. Frank and Maria moved easily among their tenants; Walter ran about and retrieved the children.

Diana remembered the remote Claude landscape she had seen from the isolation of Brandham Castle; now she felt as though she had actually stepped inside a picture, though not a Claude. Perhaps it was a rural scene by Morland or Gainsborough. Edenworth was a charmed world. Could she and her children enter such a world if she married Roger Brownlees? He was also a country landowner, though on a far smaller scale than Frank Desmond. No, she decided, it would not be the same. The atmosphere of Edenworth did not derive from the property itself, its size or the beauty of the country, and the contented prosperity of the tenants was an effect, not a cause, of the real magic, which grew out of the deep love that Frank and Maria felt for each other, their children and their home.

She now realised they were not quite such hermits as Maria had made out; they entertained large house parties here during the hunting season, with everyone riding all day and dancing all night or engaging in amateur theatricals. In the spring they themselves paid visits to various great houses on the scale of Brandham. To Maria these times seemed almost like interruptions of the domestic life she found so much more real and important.

Diana might have envied her, only she disarmed envy by being so extremely conscious of her good fortune.

"I have done nothing to deserve all this," she said, as she and Diana sauntered through the walled garden in the cool of a late afternoon. "When I hear Walter talking of the battles in Spain, and all the dreadful sufferings of the people, I feel it is selfish and wicked of me to be so happy."

Diana had asked Captain Desmond for news of Oliver's regiment; it turned out that he had served alongside them and knew many of the officers well, and this had led to a good deal of conversation about the war.

"I don't think you need feel any scruples. It is plain that your brother-in-law finds nothing here to condemn. If there was no possibility of the sort of happiness that exists at Edenworth, then England would be hardly worth fighting for."

"Yes, I suppose you are right. That is a very self-justifying reflection."

"Have you spent your whole married life here?" asked Diana, following a new train of thought.

"Apart from occasional tours and visits. We have never felt the want of a house in town. The longest I have been away from home was during the year after Francis was born, when my father was dying. He went to Bath, hoping they might find some cure for the disease, and I joined him there. We were very much attached, even more than most fathers and daughters, for my mother died young and I was their only child. Frank was so good: he spent months hanging about in Bath without a word of complaint, because he saw how badly I needed his support. Not every husband would do so much for his wife's peace of mind and the comfort of his father-in-law."

"That is very true," said Diana, whose curiosity had been satisfied.

Little Francis Desmond was now five, which meant that Sir Charles Cosway had been fatally ill four years ago, and the Desmonds had been with him. This explained why Maria had not discovered that Eliza was pregnant. Herself a young woman with a new baby, keenly interested in everything around her, she would surely have been more observant than the ailing Viscountess and her bluestocking sister. But Maria had been in Bath.

II

II

"We ought to take Mrs. Pentland to see the castle by
moonlight," Frank suggested on Monday. "That is something quite out of the common, ma'am, and the moon will
be just right this evening."

"I don't think Mrs. Pentland wants to go back to
Brandham, Frank," said Maria, perceiving Diana's air of
reluctance.

"If it's a question of avoiding Henry, he won't be there.
The Frobishers and the Dowlands were due to leave this
morning, he has no one with him now except Ledbury
and the Webbs, and they are all engaged to dine with the
Tranfords at Belmont. I expect they will stay the night on
account of the distance. They generally do."

Frank had received this news in a note from Henry
about some local business. If Eliza was going to be away,
Diana had no objection to visiting the castle, especially as
they would not be taking the children.

When they were separating to change for dinner, Maria said, "I advise you to put on something old that will not matter getting splashed."

"Surely you don't think the weather is likely to break?"

It was a calm evening after a burning hot day. The sky was as clear as glass.

"No, but we are going by boat—did we not tell you that? Brandham is not much more than a mile away by river."

They set out fairly late, giving the moon time to rise. There was a boathouse at the end of the garden. One of the undergardeners had pushed out a small, sedate craft, set the oars in place and put cushions for the ladies; Frank and his brother intended to do the rowing and had dressed for the part, in trousers and loose jackets.

They stepped aboard, handing in Maria and Diana to sit opposite them.

It was delicious on the water. The river was wide and straight here, running between level banks and green fields, past patches of rush and reed. The Desmond brothers rowed well, Walter singing an inappropriate ballad about a storm at sea; the only part he remembered properly being the chorus, which seemed to consist of the words hurly-burly, hurly-burly, repeated over and over again.

"I think that is rather a stupid song," said Maria.

"It was written by Dr. Haydn."

"Surely not the words?"

"Well, why not? Perhaps it was all the English he could manage."

Maria caught at a thin ribbon of leaf from an overhanging branch. " 'There is a willow stands aslant a brook. . . .' I wonder whether Shakespeare ever came to our river. Stratford is not so very far away."

"There are plenty of swans," said Diana, as one of the proud immaculate birds drifted disdainfully by.

"We have the two most charming swans in our boat," said Walter, smiling at the girls, whose dresses and shawls showed up with an almost luminous whiteness in the growing dusk.

"Swans, is it?" retorted Frank, assuming their native brogue. "Will you tell me I've been puffing and pulling all this way for the sake of two creatures who could just as well get out and swim?"

"You wretch, how ungallant you are!" said his wife.

They rounded a slight bend and came in sight of the castle. The sky still had a light greenish afterglow of the brilliant day, so that the power of the moon was not yet very strong, but it was beginning to cast a faint radiance across the massively curving towers and wide expanse of wall.

"What a spendid sight!" exclaimed Diana.

"It will be better later. Shall we go ashore?"

They were walking along the footpath, enjoying the beauty of the evening, when they heard movements among the trees.

A man's voice said sharply, "Who's down there?"

"Henry?"

"Good God, Frank!" Two figures came into view. "What are you all doing, creeping about in this clandestine manner? Is Walter about to besiege Brandham in the name of the Allies?"

"We wanted Mrs. Pentland to see the Castle by moonlight."

"Of course," said Henry, turning to greet Diana with exemplary good manners and a charm she did not know he possessed. "I am so glad you have such a fine night for it, Mrs. Pentland. And approaching by river, one gets far the best impression."

He and his friend Ledbury had also come out to enjoy the night landscape, and he proposed they should join forces.

"That will be very agreeable," said Maria, with a brief glance at Diana. "But why aren't you at Belmont?"

"We had got about five miles on our way when Eliza said she had the headache too badly to continue. I think she had it when we set out, and it got worse instead of better. She is certainly far from well."

"Poor Eliza, I am so sorry. Where is Horace?"

"Sulking," said his brother-in-law.

"Oh dear."

As they walked about the castle grounds and admired the play of pure silver light on ancient stone, the dark shadows cast on the pallor of the moon-washed grass, Henry attached himself to Diana and talked to her in a friendly and sensible manner. He did not make apologetic references to their previous meeting (having certainly heard from Maria that this was the last thing she wanted) but simply played the part of a good host.

"If we cross this bridge," he said, "you will see the castle reflected in the water. There—isn't that sublime? How I wish I could paint such a scene."

"Do you paint, Mr. Lambert?"

"A little, in water colour. Not very well. And it is so difficult to find the right tones for a night scene. The light is impossible anyway and the black is never really black. Still, I keep on trying. It is surprising how this place changes with the weather and season. A wisp of cloud across the moon brings an air of haunting mystery. And you should hear the nightingales singing in the trees in May."

He was a romantic, perhaps always reaching for things in his imagination that he could not quite achieve. She wondered if his fanciful decorations in the tower had fallen short of his original conception.

Presently Maria turned to say something to Henry, and Diana found herself walking next to Lord Ledbury, a chubby young man with round eyes and arched brows, which gave him a surprised expression. He asked her if she admired very old buildings.

"To look at, certainly. I am not sure that I should care to live in one."

"Neither am I. Though I think this may be partly a matter of what one is used to. My own house is excessively Palladian. So I come and stay with Lambert whenever I want to Gothicize—and one must admit that this is the real thing, no mere imitation."

"You had some authentic high-born damsels here last week," said Walter Desmond, who was on Diana's other side. "We wondered if one of them was to be added to the furnishings."

"They all tried their hardest. Miss Frobisher laughed a great deal, her sister simpered, and Emma Dowland quoted Grey in the ruins. Mrs. Frobisher and Lady Dowland both blew their daughters' trumpets to impress Eliza Webb, who looked fagged to death with the whole business, poor girl. All to no avail. None of these aspiring young ladies came anywhere near his required standard of perfection."

As he spoke, Lord Ledbury was looking at the group ahead of them: Henry between Frank and Maria. It dawned on Diana that Henry might be in love with his cousin; as she watched them she became convinced that this was so. Perhaps it was a long-standing love; they had grown up together and were the same age—which meant, of course, that he was too young for her. Too young at eighteen to compete with the masculine dash and worldly wisdom of Frank Desmond, then aged twenty-one. Diana knew that Maria had eyes for no one but Frank; she thought it very much to Henry's credit that he seemed to get on so well with them both. There was no trace of rancour or self-pity.

They had walked right round the perimeter of the castle, and Henry had just invited them all to come indoors, when a liveried servant came hurrying out of an arched doorway in one of the towers.

"Sir, we have been hunting for you everywhere! His lordship has arrived and has been asking for you this half-hour!"

"My father?" exclaimed Henry. "Here in Brandham?"

"Yes, Mr. Henry. He's come the whole way from Paraden in one day. He asked for you immediately, and when you could not be found he took a turn round the inner court, and then told Bonner to bring him the keys of the southwest tower. And after he'd been inside, he asked for you again, sir. I think he is getting a little impatient."

"Hell and damnation!" said Henry. He strode off in the direction of the archway.

"Hurly-burly, hurly-burly," Walter murmured to Diana.

The guests stood around a little uncertainly, wondering what they should do.

"Grove hasn't been here for eleven years."

"What can have induced him to descend on Henry without warning?"

For some reason they were all whispering.

"Well, it is absurd for us to skulk here as though we were trespassers," announced Maria. "We had better go in and meet my uncle."

She led the way under another arch and through a mediaeval maze of passages until they emerged into a region of tapestry-hung walls and polished boards, and Diana realised they were inside the Castle House. As they reached the foot of the fine oak staircase they could hear someone coming towards them from the opposite side. Lord Grove was apparently expressing his opinion of the southwest tower.

"Considering how moral you are, my dear Henry, it

seems very odd that you should want to turn the home of our ancestors into a Turkish brothel."

A second later father and son arrived at the staircase. Henry was annoyed, on the defensive, but Diana hardly noticed Henry. She was staring at Lord Grove. He was not the painted and corsetted wreck she had conjured up in her mind out of a Rowlandson cartoon. On the contrary, he was an active man in his forties, fit enough to run across a common flying a kite, as she had seen him do three weeks ago at Great Wickfield, when he was calling himself Mr. Wood.

She felt first hot and then cold from the shock. There was a roaring in her ears and her head felt as though it was about to burst open. Grove—Wood: the words meant the same thing, why hadn't she thought of that? And not Hop's father but Eliza's father—*he* was the Noble Client. He was the man who had been protecting her and providing for the care of her child. So it was easy to guess why he had come rushing up to Brandham.

She had seen the Desmonds greet him, as in a dumbshow. Now it was no longer possible to shrink into the tapestry.

"You are not acquainted with Lord Grove," Maria said to her in happy ignorance. "This is Mrs. Pentland, sir, who is staying with us at Edenworth."

"How do you do, Mrs. Pentland?" Grove looked straight at her without a flicker of recognition. His blue eyes were like ice.

III

"So you always tell us," said Maria; "but we are not invited to Paraden and he would have cut us dead in Bond Street last year if I hadn't given him a grand glaring

"I hope you slept well," said Maria, ensconced behind the silver tray and coffeepot. "You looked so tired when we came home last night, I was afraid you might have caught cold on the river."

Diana, taking her place at the breakfast table, said she was very much better for a good rest. In fact she had lain awake most of the night, hearing the long-case clock in the hall chime away the hours, and wrestling with a good many different emotions, all of them unpleasant.

"I wonder how they are getting on at Brandham," remarked Frank. "I told Henry his father wouldn't care for those alterations if he ever came to see them."

"He was in a shocking temper, wasn't he?" said Walter.

"They both were. Which did you mean?"

"Oh, I'm used to Henry's high flights. I was speaking of Grove. I've never seen him like that at Paraden. He can be the best of company and a capital host."

"So you always tell us," said Maria. "But we are not invited to Paraden and he would have cut us dead in Bond Street last year if I hadn't gone right up and planted myself in front of him. We are not in his good books."

"I suppose that's because you were Lady Grove's niece; he reckons you and Frank as members of the opposition. But I am not a relation. Grove gets on very well with everyone outside his own family."

"Is Mrs. Webb attached to her father?" asked Diana.

"It's curious you should ask that," said Maria, "because I believe she has been seeing a good deal of him since she grew up, in spite of knowing that he and Henry are not on good terms. As a general rule Eliza thinks Henry is right about everything."

In the watches of the night Diana had recalled Eliza coming back to Sloane Place in a glow of gratitude and relief, and saying: "I did not know he loved me so much. . . . Mama was always set against him. . . ." The man she had appealed to in her desperate need was not her estranged lover but her estranged father.

Frank said, "Just as well we have no engagements at Brandham in the next few days. I thought we might drive over to Ashton—yes, what is it, Greening?"

The butler, who had just come in, said: "Lord Grove has called, sir."

"Good God, what does he want to come here for? At this hour!"

As Grove had followed the butler into the room, he must have heard this, though he pretended not to. He stood at the end of the table looking decidedly intimidating. Both the Desmond brothers got to their feet and wished him good morning. Maria said she hoped he had come to breakfast.

"No, thank you. I breakfasted two hours ago."

"Then will you at least take a chair? It is so awkward for Frank and Walter to be obliged to eat standing up."

Grove smiled for the first time and sat down beside her; they began a somewhat stilted conversation about the weather, the state of the roads, Eliza's health. Her father said she was in a very low state. He had noticed Diana with a slight bow when he first came in, but did not speak to her directly until the end of the meal.

Frank then said, "Did you wish to see me for any special reason, my lord?"

"What I really came for," said Grove, "was the chance of a few minutes' private conversation with Mrs. Pentland."

The three Desmonds looked astonished and Diana felt herself turning scarlet with embarrassment. Maria cast her a glance of doubt and reproach; she must be recalling Henry's suspicion that the Turners' mysterious visitor was his father's mistress.

"Will you grant me an interview, ma'am?" he challenged her.

"Very well, my lord. If Mrs. Desmond does not object."

"Of course not." Maria's good manners were equal to any contingency. "If you will both come into the small saloon, you will not be disturbed."

The small saloon was a very pretty room. The deep blue walls were decorated with white garlands and the furniture was painted in the French style.

Grove stationed himself in front of the empty fireplace, where he looked even more formidable.

"Mrs. Pentland, how could you play me such a trick?" he began as soon as Maria had left them. "When I heard you had brought Hop to Brandham, I could hardly believe it, and now I find you here with the Desmonds—did you not think what the effect might be on Eliza? She is in a pitiful state, crying and saying she wants her child, and God knows how long she will be able to keep the truth from Webb in her present frame of mind. Surely you might have thought of the consequences before pursuing her to Brandham?"

"You don't suppose I came here on purpose?" retorted Diana. "How could I when I did not know who she was? Or who you were, for that matter? And if I had known, why should I want to approach your daughter? What possible motive could I have?"

"You are anxious to marry that fellow Brownlees. You were annoyed when I told you it wouldn't do. I suppose you thought Hop's mother could release you from your promise. At all events, you must have had some reason for coming to Brandham. Don't tell me it was a coincidence, for that I cannot credit."

"Of course it was not a coincidence," Diana was now so angry that her tongue was running away with her. "It was practically a foregone conclusion, thanks to the comic opera conspiracy between your lordship and Mr. Caversham, and your determination to keep me in the dark. You may recall that the house at Great Wickfield was chosen because Mrs. Caversham's niece is married to the clergyman there. It was thought desirable that I should have some neighbours I could turn to in a difficulty. Well, my lord, I did turn to them three weeks ago, after you saw fit to come down and interfere in my private concerns: I was then in the difficulty of wanting to leave the village for a few weeks, and I asked the Jacksons' advice. Mrs. Jackson suggested I should bring the children to visit her brother and his wife. Mr. Turner has recently been given the post of librarian at the Castle. On the recommendation of Mr. Caversham."

"Good heavens," interrupted Grove. "I had no idea he was Mrs. Jackson's brother. That was a serious oversight. I do beg your pardon."

"Oh, don't put yourself to the trouble, my lord. You have been keeping me for the last three years and I suppose you are entitled to insult me."

"Mrs. Pentland, I don't think I deserved that."

Diana bit her lip. She knew that her last remark had been childish and ill-bred. He had not pointed out (as he very well might have done) that she had failed to observe one of the conditions of their arrangement. If she had told Mr. Caversham she was thinking of going to Brandham, she would have been stopped. Grove had not said this; he was not petty. All the same she could not overcome a feeling of bitter humiliation.

"You are still angry," he said, watching her. "I am very sorry for having misjudged and offended you—do please try to make allowances. My son wrote a week ago to Caversham, saying that a Mrs. Pentland had come to visit the librarian here with a child who was undoubtedly a Lambert. Turner had told him, moreover, that your income was administered by Caversham. Henry was demanding to know who you were and what could be your purpose in coming. As it happened, Caversham was out of town. The letter was opened by his partner—that is to say, his real partner, whose name is Barker, not that two-faced fellow Wood. Barker knows that anything concerning you is always referred to me, so he sent the letters down to Hampshire. I was at sea in my yacht, only got home on Sunday night. I already knew that Eliza and her husband were coming up here to stay with Henry. The whole of yesterday I spent on the road, imagining what I might find at the end of my journey. I was the victim of my own folly; I should have known that you were too honourable and too discreet to risk any action that might injure my poor Eliza. I should have trusted you."

"But you never have trusted me, Lord Grove. Why should you suddenly begin?"

"Now we're getting to the root of it. You think I've treated you very badly, don't you? Perhaps you are right: you shall be the judge. When I first heard of you from Eliza, I was struck with the idea that you might be the very person to take charge of her baby. I wanted to meet you, but felt it wisest to remain *incognito*. Do you blame me for that? I knew how good you had been to Eliza, but kind-hearted women are not always the most discreet—"

"No, of course I don't blame you. At that time you could know nothing of my character. Once you decided that I was a fit person to have charge of Hop, surely there was no need to go on with the farce of calling yourself Mr. Wood? If you had told me who you were, and who Eliza was, what did you think I should do? Write gossiping letters to all my acquaintance, boasting that I had adopted the illegitimate son of the Honourable Miss Lambert?"

"No," he said coolly, "I did not think you would write letters about Miss Lambert; I thought you might feel a very strong desire to write letters to her."

"What do you mean?" she demanded.

He had remained standing in front of the fireplace. Now he sat down opposite her.

"From the morning we first met, I began to admire you for your courage in adversity, your devotion to Sukey and then to Hop, the way in which you have centred your life on the bringing-up of those two children. You have always seemed to me everything that a good mother should be. But I could not help wondering whether those very qualities might affect your feelings towards the girl whose baby had been taken from her and given to you. If you knew her name, I thought you might be tempted to write to her. Sending news of a first tooth perhaps, or a first step, enclosing a curl to go in a locket, or a little portrait. I believed that a complete break was essential for Eliza's peace of mind, but I was not sure how far you would agree with me. Perhaps I have been unduly cautious. If so, you have every right to feel ill-used, and I am very sorry."

"Of course I should not have—" Diana broke off.

Honesty compelled her to remember several occasions when she had thought about Eliza, and wished it was possible to pass on some anecdote about Hop. Would she have resisted the temptation to meddle? She could not give a positive answer, so how could she expect Grove to guess what she might have done?

"You were probably right," she conceded. "I might have acted foolishly, on a sudden whim. That is something one cannot be sure of. Does your daughter ever ask you for news of her little boy?"

"No, never. I promised her that I would tell her if he was to become dangerously ill, or if he died. Otherwise she could assume that he was safe and well. She has never asked for anything more."

"Then I am sorry that seeing me again has done her so much harm," said Diana unhappily. "I do blame myself for that. Of course I should have left Brandham as soon as I saw Mr. Henry Lambert and realised that I was stepping into a hornet's nest. If I had gone then, I should not have met Mrs. Webb."

"You must not distress yourself on that account. I went to see her in her room last night, and from what she said then, I suspect she has been silently pining for the child. If only she could have another baby, that would be the most effective cure—but it won't happen if Webb finds out he has been deceived and turns her out. We must preserve her secret if we can."

"Do you wish me to leave the district immediately?"

Grove hesitated. "You have not talked to anyone here?"

"Of course not."

He gave her a slightly enigmatic glance that she did not understand, though it slipped into the back of her consciousness, with so many other unexplained details.

"I'm afraid my entry this morning will have made things awkward for you," he said.

"I don't know how I am to face Mrs. Desmond."

"I'll talk to Maria, tell her the story I made up to satisfy Henry: that there is an irregular connection between our two families, dating back to a previous generation. I'm afraid it has to be irregular, because it can't be traced on the family tree. And it does account for Hop."

"How very ingenious. Did your son believe you?"

"Well, he didn't call me a liar to my face. At any rate Maria will believe me, so there is no need for you to feel uncomfortable, and it will seem more natural for you to stay on here a little longer. After all, it's perfectly plausible; who knows how many Noble Clients of a bygone age may have taken their troubles to Caversham's father and grandfather?"

"I hoped you had forgotten that stupid phrase," said Diana. "I invented the name to fit Hop's father. I thought our allowance was being paid as a sop to conscience by the selfish brute who had caused so much misery."

"Well, and so it was, in a sense," said Grove bleakly. "Don't you think I blame myself for what happened to Eliza? I lived apart from my wife, and neglected my children, let them grow up as though they had no father. With the result that Henry regards me as his enemy, and Eliza got into this appalling scrape. And her mother never even knew she was pregnant! I don't say that was entirely her fault, she was a sick woman by then, but the governess had left and not been replaced, my sister-in-law had her head in a book as usual, and the only person who finally recognised that poor child's plight was her fool of a maid who was too prudish to say anything about it. Yet whenever I rage against them all, I remember that they at least tried to do their duty as they saw it. I simply abandoned my children to the care of others."

He jumped up and crossed to the window, where he stood for a moment, fiddling with the latch. The rooms on

this side of the house had long Venetian windows opening
straight on to the garden.

"It's too hot indoors," he said abruptly. "Will you
come out and take the air with me?"

"Very well," she said, rising.

They stepped through the window. The morning was
still early enough for the world to look fresh and spar-
kling. They were halfway along one of the sanded paths
that ran through the formal parterre, when Grove looked
down at her and said, "I should not have dragged you out
in such a boorish fashion—you haven't a parasol or even
a hat."

"It doesn't signify. I am not affected by the sun."

Diana was wearing a pale green dress, and a very pretty cap that tied under the chin. The warm golden brown of
her hair gleamed through the fine white cambric, and loose
tendrils curled upwards round the frilled edge. She could
not have looked prettier if she had set out deliberately to
charm her companion, but she was quite unaware of this,
her mind taken up with pity for the man who seemed to
feel such agonising guilt over his failing as a father.

At the far corner of the parterre there was a strip of
grass, once a bowling alley, between high yew hedges.
They began to pace up and down inside these enclosing
hedges, hidden from the windows of the house. Diana
thought Grove's flight into the garden had been meant as
an escape from his family problems, but he reverted to
the subject immediately.

"I shall never forget the day Eliza came to find me at
my house in Arlington Street."

"It must have been a very great shock to you."

"Perhaps the most shocking thing was that I nearly refused to see her."

"Refused to see her?" repeated Diana.

"One of my servants—he was a new man, hadn't been
with me long—came in to say that there was a young lady

on the doorstep asking to see me. She had come alone, and on foot, and she claimed to be my daughter. Well you may not know this, but men in my position do get some very strange callers from time to time. Although I have no illegitimate children as far as I know, I wouldn't put it past some enterprising young woman, with a smattering of ancient scandal and a good deal of impudence, to try and pass herself off as my daughter. I told Briggs to send her packing.

"The poor fellow looked very uneasy, and said: 'Excuse me, my lord, I think it really is Miss Lambert.' So then I went out into the hall. We hadn't met for two years; I used to see her occasionally when she visited my brother's family. I was horrified, she looked so ill and distracted. She rushed into my arms and cried, 'Papa, I'm in such terrible trouble—do please help me.' "

He stopped speaking, and after a slight pause Diana said, "You did help her."

"I suppose so. She has never been happy, poor girl. She should not have married Webb. I tried to prevent it, but her mother and Henry favoured the match: they thought she was in love. I knew better, I knew she was simply running away from the past, yet what could I say? He is a perfectly respectable young man with an adequate fortune; there's nothing against him apart from the fact that he is a sullen lout who has no conversation."

"I daresay you said that, my lord," ventured Diana.

He smiled, making the effort to shake off his mood of depression. There was a bench at one end of the alley. They sat down, and he said: "There is one person who will be thankful that Mr. Wood has been unmasked: Caversham. The impersonation has always horrified him."

"I expect he thought it was beneath your dignity."

"Possibly. I'm sure he thought it was beneath his own, to have such a ramshackle associate. Do you remember, that first morning in Lincoln's Inn, our having a most interesting discussion as to whether you should get rid of the wet-nurse and buy a goat? I thought old Caversham would have an apoplexy."

They were still laughing at this ridiculous memory when Henry came silently round the corner of the yew hedge and stopped, about six feet away from them.

"I thought I should surprise you together!" he said accusingly.

"You have not surprised me, Henry," said Grove. "You may have surprised Mrs. Pentland, who is not accustomed to your bad manners. To me, I'm sorry to say, they are only too familiar."

The young man flushed. Having his own word thrown back at him in its other meaning, he had somehow lost the thread of what he was going to say next. He glanced suspiciously at Diana and then at his father.

"This long-standing family claim which you say we have always honoured—I never heard of it before."

"I dare say not."

"If you and Caversham always knew about it, why have I never been told?"

"You are not the head of the family. Yet."

"Well, it seems damned odd to me," muttered Henry, rebellious and unconvinced. "Why were you both laughing just now?"

He spoke with a deep distrust, as though their laughter was a proof of something disgraceful.

"Why the devil shouldn't we laugh?"

"When you pretend to be meeting for the first time—"

"Mr. Lambert," said Diana quickly, "there are some men who can make a woman laugh on a very recent and slight acquaintance, and your father is one of them. There is no mystery about that."

Which was true if a little specious. She and Grove had been laughing about an incident which had amused them both at their very first encounter.

Henry cast her an eloquent glance, more in sorrow than in anger, with his brilliant hazel eyes—Hop's eyes.

"There is never any mystery, ma'am, where my father is concerned. I beg your pardon for disturbing you."

He bowed and walked away.

"Damn his impudence," said Grove, preparing to follow him. "We shall have to tell him the truth."

"You cannot do that, sir. Eliza—"

"I'm trying to save Eliza's marriage and prevent a public scandal: this would make no difference. The boy won't betray his sister."

"But she is so anxious that he should not find out. She is afraid he will turn against her."

"Yes, I know," admitted Grove. "And I fear she may be right. He's cursed with the blinding egotism of all romantics. If a man fills his mind with impossibly elevated sentiments and false heroics, he can never come to terms with ordinary fallible mortals. Henry goes about with his head in the Alps and his feet in the Catacombs—what are you laughing at?"

"You paint such an exact picture!"

"Unluckily all stupidity has to be paid for, generally by the wrong person. Because Henry could not bear the truth about his sister he can square accounts with reality only by believing—what he does believe—about you."

"It doesn't matter." Diana looked carefully away from Grove. The smooth green shapes of the garden shimmered in the heat haze. "Nothing we can tell him now is likely to alter your son's opinion of me, and in any case he can do me no harm. Clearly one must accept the lesser of two evils."

"What am I to say to such generosity? I ought to refuse, but I cannot, for Eliza's sake. And you have such an admirable sense of proportion; you are the first person ever to describe me as a lesser evil."

IV

Whatever Henry might think of his father's story, Maria believed it without question. Diana thought she noticed one or two speculating glances from the Desmond brothers—speculating but not censorious. She knew that they moved in a world which allowed a married woman as many lovers as she pleased, provided she was discreet. And according to their rules she was being discreet; her arrival in Brandham with Hop had come as a surprise, but she had made no claims and no scenes—it was Henry who had a tendency to make scenes, and this was what embarrassed his relations.

As for her own feelings, Diana had realised that she hardly minded being mistaken for Grove's mistress, now she knew who he was. It was a shaming thing to admit, even to oneself, but she could not help it.

Next morning Maria received a note from the Castle.

"It's from Eliza," she said, reading it with a slight

frown. "She wants to come and dine with us—in fact she has practically invited herself. How extraordinary she is! She has refused us so often before that I have given up asking her. Now she makes me appear as a very negligent neighbour who has to be hinted into good manners."

"I'm sure she does not think you have neglected her," said Frank.

"Well, I hope not. We shall have to ask them all, and I suppose Grove and Henry will carry on their feud and it will all be most uncomfortable. Why are my relations so tiresome?"

"Everyone's relations are tiresome," said Frank, grinning, "only Walter's and mine live in Ireland, which is much more convenient."

Diana knew why Eliza wanted to dine at Edenworth, and found the prospect alarming until she realised that Grove would manage to stop her if he thought it was necessary; he was in charge of the situation now. So she could listen calmly while Frank and Maria discussed plans and fixed on Saturday for the dinner party.

As soon as the invitation had been despatched, Diana and Maria went into the garden, where they spent the rest of the morning looking at Maria's flowers and shrubs and deciding which would be suitable for Diana to grow in her restricted space at Palfreys and in the Essex clay. Maria was a keen gardener and promised her a great many cuttings.

They were returning to the house for luncheon when they caught sight of a curricle in the avenue.

"Callers!" exclaimed Maria, as though they were a tribe of hostile American Indians.

"I think it is your cousins."

"Good God, I believe you are right. Henry and Eliza: what can they be doing here? We did not expect them today. Do you think I misread her letter?"

It soon transpired that the visitors had come on the spur of the moment—at least Henry had, though Diana guessed he had been manoeuvred into this by his sister.

"We've been over at Tufton, inspecting the new canal," she said, jumping down from the curricle, animated and almost pretty. "And it was all taking such a time; Papa is so interested in locks and all that kind of thing, so I said to Henry, why should we not drive back by Edenworth?"

Henry said: "There was no point in letting Lizzie stand about in the heat. I thought it would do her more good to come here."

He smiled down at his sister from the curricle, and she smiled up at him. Diana had never seen them together; their visible affection brought out the best in them both. Eliza was wearing a sprig muslin dress, a pink silk spencer, and a white straw bonnet trimmed with a wreath of artificial flowers—apple blossom and wild roses. Once again Diana was surprised to remember how young she still was.

"I hope you do not mind us coming," she said to Maria. "Your kind invitation to dinner was delivered just before we left the Castle, but unfortunately Papa has fixed on Saturday as the day we must visit my Aunt Augusta at Broadleigh. I am not sure why."

"Simply to give himself the pleasure of having his own way," said Grove's heir. "No one must ever arrange anything except his lordship."

"Henry, that is unjust," protested Eliza. "I am sure Papa has good reasons for everything he does. At least they seem good to him."

"Oh, you always stand up for him, God knows why. What has he ever done for you?"

Eliza caught Diana's eye and looked hastily away.

"Well, we've given him the slip this morning," added Henry with satisfaction.

"I am sorry to disappoint you," remarked Maria, "but there is another carriage coming up the avenue and I'm pretty sure it is your landau."

"For pity's sake!" Henry craned round to see, and said something very unfilial not quite under his breath. He remained perfectly still on the high-sprung seat of the curricle watching the approach of the landau. Grove was on the box, with a groom beside him; Ledbury and Horace Webb were in the open carriage. They all looked hot and glum.

"Well done, sir," said Henry. "You have hunted us successfully over five miles of turnpike road! I suppose you thought I was not able to take care of my sister."

Maria interrupted quickly and asked them all to lunch.

"That's very kind of you, my dear," said Grove, deciding to ignore his son's insolence. He handed the reins to the groom and stepped down. "Heavy, isn't it? I think the weather's going to break. Have you got all your hay in?"

"What on earth made you go off like that without telling me?" Horace Webb asked his wife in a complaining tone. "I couldn't imagine what had become of you."

"I suppose you thought I'd fallen in the canal," she retorted.

A trapped expression had come back into her face, and Diana thought she was near the end of her tether. As they walked towards the house she managed to say quietly, "Of course I know why you are here. I will take you upstairs later to see the little boy. The children are all having their midday rest at present. Only try to remain calm. You do not wish to draw attention to yourself and your interest in Hop."

They were all moving into the house, and Eliza had time for only a brief smile before Maria took her away to wash off the dust of the morning's drive.

The usual cold ham and the sandwich tray would not

suffice. A light luncheon for nine people was being hurriedly assembled in the dining room; it was extraordinary what Maria's cook could produce at short notice. While the guests were waiting Diana spoke to Grove. She felt obliged to let Eliza see Hop, since this was what she wanted so desperately. She hoped he did not disapprove?

"Not if she can keep some command over her feelings," he said, doubtfully. "I have already promised to bring her to see you at Palfreys some time in the autumn. I'd rather have waited till then."

It was impossible to say more, for Henry was watching them. Frank and Walter Desmond had now arrived, and as they all gathered informally round the dining room table Maria came into the room alone.

Diana felt a prickle of apprehension down her spine.

"What has happened to Mrs. Webb?" She hoped the question did not sound too inquisitive.

"She says she never takes lunch now," replied Maria. "I left her talking to Watson—my maid, you know, who was with me at the Castle, before I married."

In spite of the informality a listless air hung over the party. After the beautiful weather of the last fortnight, the sky was now overcast, the sun dulled. Diana seated with her back to the long windows, saw the garden reflected in the blue-grey surface of the glass over the fireplace; it seemed remote and lifeless.

Grove was seated next to Captain Walter Desmond, always his champion at Edenworth, who was happily recalling visits to Paraden.

"Did you give another feast for your tenants this Whitsun, sir?"

"We hold one every year."

"Lord Grove's Whitsun feasts are the most glorious occasions," Walter informed the company at large. "He provides a regular banquet for his tenants, and there is a band and a cricket match, dancing on the grass and a firework display in the evening. It is meant for the estate people, but everyone comes from miles around, gentry and cottagers alike; I believe no one is ever turned away. He ends by feeding half the county."

Diana was fascinated and enlightened by this portrait of Grove as a great landowner. Here was the man who had taken such care to see that she had a comfortable home, who had brought Hop a kite and insisted on flying it for him. A generous, unaffected man who liked people to enjoy themselves and knew how to make sure that they did.

Henry's response was in a different key. "One hardly supposes that the more respectable neighbours care for such a display. It must appear as a reflection on their charity to their own poor dependents."

"What a killjoy you are, Henry," said his father. "I don't regard our Whitsun feast as an opportunity for doling out charity to the poor—that is done separately and privately. I like to entertain my neighbours of every rank in society. They don't have to be starving, or even particularly deserving. It's a sorry heart that was never allowed to rejoice over some unmerited pleasure. But you cannot admit such a dangerous sentiment. What will you give them when I am dead? A bowl of gruel and a sermon?"

Hot with mortification, Henry began to justify himself, "I did not mean—I merely said—"

"Henry is very good to your tenants at Brandham, my lord," put in Frank, standing up for his friend.

At the same moment Ledbury chimed in with a neutral comment on village cricket, and there was a general conversation about country amusements.

"And what do you think of these important topics?" Maria asked Horace Webb, who had been eating his cold chicken in self-imposed isolation at the end of the table.

"I don't know anything about them. I'm not a landed proprietor."

There was an uneasy pause. All the men looked down their noses, united by a single thought. We have always pretended that this fellow was one of us, their silence seemed to say; it is simply his own ill-breeding which makes the difference so plain.

Diana was at once irritated by Horace Webb and unexpectedly sorry for him. She too was an outsider, here on preference.

She moved to the chair next to him and asked him to choose her a peach from the pyramid of fruit piled high on a gold and white china tazza. He selected one that had a velvet skin flushed on one cheek to perfect ripeness, and asked if he should peel it for her. He had the manners and *savoir faire* of a gentleman; it was his constant bad temper which made him appear so graceless—unlike Henry, whose moods, however outrageous, went so well with his romantic good looks that even his rudeness to his father had a misleading air of gallant defiance.

Diana set herself to charm Horace Webb. So he preferred the town to the country? Whereabouts in London did they live?

"In Grosvenor Street, ma'am. Where else would you suppose?"

She thought this was a snub, and then realised that the irony was not directed at her. She knew he was said to be clever, and by prodding a little she found that he was interested in all new discoveries and scientific inventions.

"The sort of thing that no one at Brandham cares about. One cannot presume to mention steam engines in a Gothic castle."

"I hear your father-in-law is interested in the Tufton Canal."

"Naturally. It runs through his land."

What a hedgehog you are, she thought. It was most

unfortunate that Eliza, so anxious to marry, should have received her first offer from such a difficult and touchy young man. But why had he asked Eliza?

There was a timid tap on the door, which opened a few inches, and Nancy's head appeared apologetically in the gap.

"Excuse me, ma'am," she said to Diana, in a nervous, faltering voice, "but have you brought Master Hop downstairs? We can't find him anywhere."

Diana was gripped by a sudden terror. A delayed premonition, as though she had known all along that there was a calamity hanging over them and the shape it would take. She ran out of the room without a word and started up the front stairs, with Nancy at her heels.

"Where did you see him last? How long ago?"

Nancy began to explain. She and the two children were sharing a bedroom on the top floor, near the Desmond children's nursery, and this answered well enough at night, but in the middle of the day, when they were supposed to rest, Sukey and Hop would talk and keep each other awake. So Hop had been resting in a dressing room further down the corridor. Diana knew this already. Nancy told her that Hop had been so quiet she thought he must be asleep. A few minutes ago she had gone in to get him up, and he was not there.

"He didn't fall out of the window, ma'am. There was barely an inch open at the top—I'm always careful about the windows. Only how he could have opened and shut the door, the handle being so stiff—and then there are his clothes."

"What about his clothes?"

"I took them off for him to lie down, yet they've gone, too. And he isn't able to dress himself."

That settles it, thought Diana. They had reached the first floor landing, and a middle-aged woman in black was standing in one of the doorways. This was Watson, Maria's dresser.

"Do you know where Mrs. Webb has gone?" Diana asked her. "She came up to see you, I believe?"

"Did she not join the party in the dining room, ma'am? That's what she meant to do—half an hour ago, it must have been."

Half an hour. Diana turned and ran downstairs again, to the astonishment of Nancy, who had been hurrying on to the top floor. Diana knew that Hop and Eliza were not to be found near the nursery. She ran through the hall, into the little blue saloon, and out by the venetian window, across the ornamental parterre, remembering a dark February day in Hans Town and Mrs. Barridge talking of Westminster Bridge. Once she was beyond the projection of the yew hedge, she could see a long straight stretch of the river in both directions.

There was not a soul in sight.

She heard a step behind her, and a hand closed firmly on her arm.

"Don't be afraid," said Grove. "She cannot have gone that way, or they would still be within sight. She would either have to carry the boy or walk at his pace."

"If she had gone straight into the water—"

"My dear, there are half a dozen gardeners about the place who would have seen and heard her."

"Yes, you are right. I'm making a fool of myself. But she is so unhappy, and I cannot see how else she could hope to keep him with her—it is so irrational."

"She is not rational, poor girl. That does not mean she will try to harm him."

They went back to the house and were soon surrounded by people asking questions. For an interminable time, in fact, about twenty minutes, Diana felt that everyone was talking at once and talking nonsense. The house was searched from attic to cellar without a trace being found of either Hop or Eliza.

"It must be a coincidence," said Horace Webb, who could not imagine his fretful wife with her perpetual headaches seeking the company of a three-year-old child.

"Why should she take him?" demanded Henry. "That's what I can't make out."

"They say that a childless woman will sometimes do such things," Maria sounded doubtful.

"My sister is not mad!"

"No, no! Certainly not. I never suggested—"

"Adam has seen them!" announced Frank, bursting into the hall and shepherding before him a weatherbeaten old man in corduroys. "He was scything the grass verge in the avenue—tell Mrs. Desmond what you told me, Adam."

The old man touched his forelock, gazed round his audience and addressed himself to Maria.

"The young lady, ma'am—Miss Lambert that was—she had this baby with her, no bigger'n Master Charley. And he called out to me, 'I'm a-going on the stagecoach.' Well, it seemed a rum go, his lordship's daughter, and with such a little chap, but he was as pleased as punch and no mistake."

"Going on the stagecoach?"

"I'll follow them," said Henry immediately. "I'll soon overtake them in the curricle."

"May I come with you, Mr. Lambert?" asked Diana.

He was already on the doorstep, and glanced round as though he could not at first remember why she should want to come. Then he recollected himself.

"By all means, Mrs. Pentland. You must be as anxious as we are."

Diana would rather have had Grove with her on this expedition and she saw that he wished to go after his daughter, but Henry had volunteered, and it would be futile to waste time arguing. So Grove restrained himself, saying merely, "The curricle won't be big enough. You had better take the landau."

Henry was in such a hurry that for once he did not bother to disagree with his father.

As they went spinning down the avenue, Diana seated on the box beside him, she asked how far it was to the nearest coaching stage. She knew that no public coaches came through Edenworth village, which was not on a main road.

"The Cat and Fiddle is a quarter of a mile from the Edenworth lodge. That's about three-quarters of a mile in all, starting from the house. Could your little boy walk so far?"

"I am not sure," she said uncertainly.

"I doubt if Eliza can, in her present state. We'll soon catch up with them. . . . Mrs. Pentland, what can induce a young woman to act in such an extraordinary way? I know she is very unhappy, though I don't know why, for she was dead set on marrying Webb; my mother and I thought they were fond of each other. And even a disappointing marriage is no excuse for stealing another woman's child."

Diana murmured something noncommittal. She saw the puckered frown of perplexity as Henry stared down the avenue over the heads of his horses, and he reminded her so vividly of Hop, trying to work out some arrangement of his toy soldiers. Darling Hop, where was he now? Where was Eliza taking him? To abduct a child, even if it was her own child, and to run away from her husband and friends without warning or preparation, she must indeed have reached a point bordering on insanity.

They had now arrived at the imposing iron gates of Edenworth Hall, and the lodgekeeper's wife came out to let them through. She was always on the alert for the sound of carriages, but paid little attention to people on foot; she had seen nothing of Hop or Eliza.

The road outside was no more than a lane running between Edenworth village and the turnpike road. Henry turned to the right. It had now come on to rain.

"You're getting wet," he said. "Would you like to ride in the back? I can put up the head."

"It doesn't matter. I'd much rather you pressed on."

They bumped and swayed over the bad surface. Diana clung to the seat and peered from side to side at the hedges and trees, hoping at every bend in the lane to see the longed-for sight of tall Eliza and tiny Hop. There was no one about. The rain was pelting down by now, and Diana's summer dress, as thin as paper, was soon soaked through.

They followed the winding lane to its final corner and were confronted by the tollgate placed here by the authority of the Brandham and Tufton Turnpike Trust.

"Come on, come on," muttered Henry impatiently, as they waited for the pikeman to come out from his little sentry-box of a cottage.

Diana leant forward hopefully, trying to get a good view of the crossroads, but this was not easy, for the tollgate was set a little way back in the lane. She could see the back of a large white building which Henry said was the Cat and Fiddle Inn, but it was impossible to see the front, where passengers would wait for the coaches.

The pikeman came out into the rain with a sack over his head.

"Have you had a young lady and a little boy go through this gate in the last half-hour?" asked Henry.

"I don't recall. What sort of a carriage, sir?"

"They were on foot."

"Then they'd go through free. Can't keep a tally of all

the walking females traipsing back and forth all day long, silly hens!"

"This was a lady, my good fellow," said Henry imperiously. "You must have noticed her."

The pikeman had the invaluable English talent for avenging himself on his superiors by pretending to be even stupider than they expected. He just stood there looking obtuse. When Henry took out his purse and commanded him to open the gate, he said very slowly that he would have to write out a ticket. Grove would have managed him better.

"He'll be all day," said Diana. "I'll go through on foot myself, and you can follow."

She did not wait for him to object; she jumped down and ducked under the gate. Once she was round the corner she could see the front of the inn. No sign of the runaways. Still, she had hardly expected them to be standing outside in the rain. She splashed across the yard and into the porch of the Cat and Fiddle.

"Is there anyone about?"

A servant came out of the coffee room and eyed her with concern. "Has there been an accident, ma'am?"

"I hope not," said Diana fervently. "I am looking for a lady and a little boy. Are they here perhaps?"

The man shook his head. He had not seen any ladies with little boys, and there were no travellers here at present.

"What was the last coach to stop here?"

"The London to Manchester, ma'am. Went through shortly after two o'clock. They picked up several passengers which I didn't take much note of, being as I was waiting on a party from a post-chaise at the time."

She thanked him and turned to go. Eliza and Hop could not have reached the Cat and Fiddle early enough to catch the Manchester coach—unless they had been given a lift along the lane in some farm cart or gig. This was something she and Henry had not considered, yet it was perfectly possible. Otherwise where could they be? There was nowhere here for them to shelter except the inn. She gazed across the rain-swept desolation of the intersecting roads and felt a dreadful weight of apprehension at the idea of Hop being carried further and further away from her.

He might have set out gaily enough, but once he became tired his spirits would flag. He would ask for her and for Nancy. When he realised that he was in a totally unknown world among strangers, the adventure would become a nightmare. Eliza knew nothing about looking after children, nor about travelling on a public coach and without servants to wait on her. What sort of a scrape would they get into?

Shoulders braced against the rain, Diana was turning back towards the tollgate when something made her pause and glance to her right along the turnpike road. Two figures were trudging wearily towards the crossroads: such a bedraggled and dejected pair that her eye summed them up automatically as the sort of pathetic vagrants who could always be found wandering on any highway. Then she looked again, and at the same moment the smaller figure broke into a stumbling trot, sobbing as he ran.

"Mama! Mama!"

Diana ran too. She caught him up in her arms, a disgracefully dirty little object, wailing with anguish and fright and some dreadful experience he wanted to relate and could not force into words while he was crying so hard.

"You're safe now, my pet," she kept reassuring him. "You're safe with Mama. Don't cry any more. No one's going to hurt you."

Hop choked back his sobs long enough to get out what he was trying to say.

"We never seed the 'tagecoach!"

"Didn't you, my love? Never mind that now."

She clasped him tightly; the contact of his small body sent waves of relief flooding through her. Now she was able to attend to Eliza, who was a pitiful sight indeed. There were great smears of mud running down from the shoulder of her pink spencer to the hem of her dress, which was badly torn. Her smart bonnet was limp and sopping, the wreath of flowers had come unpinned and hung down with an air of ludicrous dissipation. Her face was white, exhausted, and despairing.

"I can't stop him crying," she said. "He got so tired. I did carry him as far as I could."

"But what's happened to you? Where did you come from? You weren't in the lane."

"We took a short cut across the park. I thought we could get to the pike road and back in half an hour and never be missed. I thought he could see all the coaches he wanted."

They were at the door of the Cat and Fiddle; Diana took them inside. The servant was most solicitous; he was now convinced there had been an accident. Diana sent him for some brandy.

Eliza collapsed on a settle in the empty coffee room, and Diana sat down opposite her, still hugging Hop, whose sobs had gradually subsided.

"Do you mean to tell me you were simply bringing Hop here to look at the coaches?"

"Please don't be angry with me," begged Eliza, her lip trembling. "I know it was very stupid and wrong of me. I didn't mean to do anything so—I only meant to take a peep at him, and then I found him alone, such a bright confiding little fellow, and when he asked me to take him to see the stagecoach—"

" 'Tagecoach!" bellowed Hop, remembering his grievance.

"Stop that silly noise at once," said Diana severely.

The little wretch began to ingratiate himself, murmuring, "Dear Mama, dear Mama," and pressing warm, wet kisses on her cold, wet face. Diana could not resist the pleasure of cuddling him, so blessedly restored to her, though she felt that this display of affection must be dreadful for poor Eliza, who had wanted to give her son a simple treat because it was the first thing he had ever asked of her. She had misjudged the distance; she had not taken that short cut for some years, and then probably on horseback. The rain had started, Hop had begun to cry—like all small children, he hated being uncomfortable—and once they left the park, Eliza had lost her way. They had been obliged to cross a deep ditch: Eliza had tried to carry Hop over, and they had both fallen in. It was a ridiculous odyssey, and in its underlying cause tragic.

"He kept asking for his mama," said Eliza miserably. "And of course he meant you, not me."

"The word has no exact meaning to a child. It is simply the person he is used to."

Eliza sipped her brandy in a dejected silence. Then, a little revived, she took in the oddness of the situation. "What are you doing here—good God, they are not all out searching for us?"

"No, just your brother and I. We came to fetch you in the landau—and I can't think what's become of him. I do trust he hasn't murdered that Pikey!"

"Oh, lord, have I got to face Henry? I had so much rather it was Papa."

"So should I," said Diana frankly. "But don't be alarmed. Say as little as possible and leave it all to me."

She could hear voices in the passage. A moment later Henry came striding in. He looked intently at his sister, as though trying to determine whether she had gone out of her mind, and apparently decided that she hadn't (What did he expect? Straws in the hair?) for he spoke in quite an ordinary voice.

"My dearest Lizzie, what possessed you to lead us on a wild goose chase! And what have you done to yourself, for heaven's sake?"

"Mrs. Webb has had a very trying afternoon," said Diana quickly.

Conscious of Eliza on the verge of tears, she explained away the ill-fated expedition as lightly as she could. Henry looked completely baffled by his sister's silliness, though he was too fond of her to say so, while she was in such obvious distress. He transferred his attention to Hop, and Diana saw the angry frown of recollection as he studied the little boy, staring pointedly at his left hand. It seemed astonishing to Diana that he still had not grasped the truth. Then it struck her that Eliza had one powerful safeguard: none of her relations could suspect her of having an illegitimate child, because they would not believe it possible that she had gone through her whole pregnancy unnoticed.

Henry was saying they must drive back to Edenworth immediately, before the girls in their thin dresses caught cold. All being well, thought Diana, the episode had done no lasting harm.

PART FIVE

Truth Will Out

I

When they got back to the Hall the entire party hurried to meet them, and there had to be more explanations. However, Diana and Eliza were both so wet that these plans were curtailed so that the women could go upstairs and change.

Diana went first to the nursery with Hop, who was none the worse for his adventure, only very dirty, which he rather enjoyed, and in a fair way to being spoilt by all the fuss.

Nancy hugged him, the little Desmonds came running up to stare, their old nurse clucked over him and called him a poor little mite, while Sukey gave a cry of anguish.

"Oh, poor, poor Hop. Were the gipsies cruel to you?"

"I went in a landau," said Hop importantly. He had forgotten his disappointment over the stagecoach.

"Gipsies?" Diana glanced enquiringly at Nancy.

"She persuaded herself that the gipsies had taken him, ma'am. I was afraid she would make herself ill."

"My love, there weren't any gipsies. No one has been cruel. Hop just went for a walk in the rain and got lost."

As she comforted the child and watched her pathetic little woe-begone face, Diana felt a pang of guilt. She had rushed off in search of Hop, leaving Sukey to suffer all the terrors conjured up by some stupid servants' prattle, half-understood. Thinking of her adopted son, she had neglected her own daughter—Oliver's daughter. It was too bad. Hop was a true Lambert, with all their patrician egotism, their tendency to seize the centre of the stage, and for the moment Diana felt exasperated by the whole Lambert family.

Eventually she went to change. It was a relief to peel off her sopping muslin and put on a yellow gauze dress that she could wear for dinner, and to enjoy the comfort of clean, dry shoes and stockings. Her damp curls were straggling round her face and neck; they needed a good deal of dexterity to comb them into place. All this took time, and when she was finally ready to go downstairs again the house seemed very quiet. As she approached the large saloon where they assembled before dinner, she decided the Lamberts must be on their way back to the Castle by now. She hoped they were. Even the pleasure of seeing Grove would not compensate for the awkwardness and strain of the whole situation.

She opened the door and found the room was full of people.

At the centre of a motionless group, and the focus of everyone's attention, however much they tried to dissemble, Eliza sat bolt upright on a sofa, her hands in her lap, fidgeting with her rings. Maria had lent her a dress which was too short for her. Her hair still hung in wispy strands and her face was stripped of all the artifice and self-possession with which civilised men and women disguise their private fears. Diana wondered whether Grove would get her home before she broke down; she could not imagine why they were still at Edenworth. Surely Maria had not invited them all to dinner?

She must have shown her astonishment, for Grove said, "We are on the point of leaving, Mrs. Pentland. Desmond has offered to lend us a closed carriage. The landau is pretty well waterlogged."

Frank murmured, "I cannot think why they are taking so long."

He offered Diana a chair and said, "I hope your little boy is none the worse for his wetting?"

"Why should he be?" demanded Eliza, breaking in before Diana could answer. "Children are not made of sugar."

Diana was too sorry for Eliza to let herself be annoyed. Maria was not prepared to pass such a stupid remark from the person who had caused all the trouble.

"You would not talk like that if you had ever sat up all night with a sick child—would she, Mrs. Pentland? But then, you could never have been so thoughtless if you had a child of your own."

"Well, you are wrong, Maria," retorted Eliza in a shrill, aggressive voice. "I have got a child. Hop is my son."

They stared at her, not accepting this extraordinary statement, but convinced by now that she must be deranged.

"Elizabeth—don't!" said Grove, speaking sharply to curb her rising hysteria. He got up and moved towards her, but Henry stepped in front of him.

"You leave her alone. I won't have you bullying her." He stooped over Eliza. "My dear little sister, you are ill, you don't know what you are saying."

"Yes, I do. He is my baby."

"Eliza, he cannot be," Maria began to reason with her, kindly but firmly. "Mrs. Pentland is Hop's mother, and besides, he is three years old. How could you possibly have a child—"

"Shall I tell you, Maria. Do you want to hear?"

"No!" said Grove again.

"Because of what happened to me in this house! Because Frank made love to me here when you were in Bath with your father—"

"Lizzie!" exclaimed Frank Desmond. He was standing behind the sofa, looking down at her over the high back. All eyes were turned on him now, though viewing him perhaps as a mere victim of Eliza's delusions. It was Frank himself who finally gave the game away.

"You never told me there was going to be a child!"

"Why should I? You wouldn't have cared."

"It isn't true!" protested Henry, gazing at his sister in horror. "I don't believe it."

"You don't know how wicked I am," cried Eliza. "I wanted him to run away with me, I always loved him— more than she did—" The words were lost in high, breathless sobs, as she rocked herself backwards and forwards into a frenzy of despair. "And I gave away my baby—that was the worst of all."

Diana went to her, saying: "You did what was best for him, my dear. And everything else was over years ago. You must not dwell on the past."

It was instinctive to put an arm round the weeping girl and hold her as though she too was a child. Around them were the sounds of angry argument, and then a scuffle: Henry wanted to set on Frank with his bare fists and the other men were restraining him.

The butler came in, soft-footed, to announce: "The carriage is at the door, sir."

Everyone froze—as though they were playing grandmother's steps, thought Diana, who was feeling slightly hysterical herself.

When the man had gone, Grove said doubtfully that he was not sure if Eliza was in a fit state to make the journey.

A voice Diana hardly recognised, said, "I won't have that trollop in my house a moment longer than I have to."

Erect and pale, her eyes fiery, her small white teeth biting her lower lip, the gentle Maria was like a vixen at bay.

"Very well," said Grove. "We'll go at once. Come, Lizzie."

Eliza clung to Diana's hands, saying, "Don't leave me."

Grove cast her an imploring glance. "I hardly like to ask—"

"Yes, of course I'll drive to Brandham with her, Lord Grove."

As they led the trembling Eliza out of the saloon, Diana was aware of isolated figures in the shadows of the dark afternoon: of a distracted Frank trying to plead with Maria, who turned away her vixen mask. Of Henry sitting with his head in his hands. Walter and Lord Ledbury, embarrassed spectators, were talking in low voices at the far end of the room. And the most solitary of all, perhaps: Horace Webb, shoulders hunched, hands in pockets, staring sullenly at the floor. In all the uproar she had not heard him say a word.

Diana and Eliza travelled alone in the Desmonds' comfortable chaise. The four men of the party were to bring back the curricle and the landau. Diana did not try to talk; she thought Eliza was better left to herself as she recovered from the emotional storms of the day. . . . So Frank Desmond was Hop's father. That was a complication Diana had never foreseen.

She had not thought much lately about the identity of

Eliza's lover. He had interested her once because she was under the mistaken impression that Hop took after him in looks, and also that he was the Noble Client who wielded such power in the background of her own life. When she discovered that looks and money alike came from the Lamberts, she had lost interest in the unknown man whom she never expected to meet.

Yet who would have had a better opportunity to seduce a young girl, not yet out, than a near neighbour who was also a connection by marriage? The solution now seemed obvious, and much more shocking.

"She always patronised me," said Eliza presently, leaning back in her corner of the chaise. "I did not mind so much when we were both in the schoolroom. But then she grew up into a young lady; she took Henry away from me, and Frank, whom I'd fallen headlong in love with at fourteen. She made them both moon after her in that stupid fashion and I was left behind. She's always had everything I wanted, and this afternoon I could not stand any more. Always boasting about her fine family, when my poor little boy was something to be ashamed of."

"Good God! I had not considered—Francis and Charley Desmond are Hop's brothers."

"Yes, isn't it strange?" said Eliza with the detachment of extreme weariness. "Not that it makes much odds. I used to think such ties were indestructible; when I was lonely and sick to death of my own company and Horace ignored me, I used to think, I have a son, a little child of my own, if he was here we should love each other and be happy. Only it's not true. Hop will never love me in that way. If he ever knew I was his mother, he would despise me for parting with him. And as long as he doesn't know, I am just a tiresome female who doesn't understand about boys. And either way, I've lost my baby. No one can give me back those three years."

Although Diana tried to say something consoling, she

knew Eliza was right. The fiasco of her afternoon's adventure had been a bitter disappointment and it was probably this, rather than the desire to hit back at Maria, which had brought on her hysterical outburst. Disillusioned about the sacred bonds of motherhood, deprived of her poor little comforting dream, she no longer cared what became of her, and all Grove's efforts had been wasted.

She seemed to be thinking along the same lines, for after a moment she said, "Mrs. Pentland—Diana—I know I have behaved very ungratefully to you and Papa, after all the trouble you have taken—"

"You don't have to apologise, my dear. I know how hard it has been for you, and I am sure your father understands."

"There will be a great scandal now, I suppose. Horace will probably divorce me and I don't care if he does. Except that Papa and Henry will mind so dreadfully."

Diana did not think that Horace Webb could get an Act through Parliament to divorce his wife for something she had done before their marriage. But he might have the marriage declared null, on the grounds that he had been deceived over the chastity of his bride. That would be just as unpleasant for the Lambert and Desmond families, if not worse. There was a great deal of trouble and unhappiness ahead for them all, especially if Horace Webb was vindictive, and she was very much afraid he would be. And all this because she had brought Hop to Brandham.

If only I had never come near the place, she thought remorsefully, as they drove over the bridge and through the archway, and she was reminded of her arrival at the Librarian's House, not quite a fortnight ago. How delightfully romantic these towers had seemed to her then, when she thought them and their inhabitants quite remote from anything painful or disagreeable in the present day.

This time they drew up outside the Castle House. Diana went in with Eliza, and upstairs with her to a large bedroom on the first floor where her maid Parker was waiting.

Parker was the same maid who had been with Eliza all along, the only person who had realised that she was pregnant. At that time she had proved a broken reed. However, she was really devoted to her mistress, knew all her secrets, and was completely trustworthy; she was well fitted to take charge when Diana had quickly explained to her what had happened at Edenworth.

Parker shook her head and declared that it was no more than she'd expected all along, her poor dear lady being in such low spirits. She then said what she thought of men in general and That Wicked Brute in particular, and soon began very competently to put Eliza to bed.

Diana felt she was in the way, so she said good night at once. Outside the bedroom a tall footman in a powdered wig was waiting for her.

"His lordship's compliments, ma'am, and I was to show you to the small library."

He led her through the picture gallery, down a different staircase, and into this deceptively named apartment, which was about the size of the whole ground floor at Palfreys. Tooled leather volumes, gleaming with gold, ran eight shelves high round every wall. A Pembroke table in the centre was set for a meal. Grove came forward to greet her. He had found time to change his coat and looked reasonably composed.

"I thought you would prefer to dine in here, rather than join our entirely masculine party. The carriage will take you back to Edenworth when you are ready."

"Oh, but you should not have troubled. . . ." She began the kind of polite protest which would have been obligatory in a more modest household, realised that this was ridiculous and stopped.

Grove smiled. "You must allow me to return your hospitality. That's all, Thomas. I'll wait on Mrs. Pentland myself."

"Very good, my lord." The footman withdrew.

"The fact is," said Grove, "I don't think you would find it very agreeable dining with my son and my son-in-law this evening." He made a slight grimace. "How did you leave Eliza?"

"Very forlorn, I'm afraid. But she is perfectly calm."

"Well, that is an improvement. May I help you to some salmon? And a little cucumber salad?"

"Thank you, I don't care what I eat. I am not hungry. My lord, I feel so dreadfully that it is my fault this calamity has overtaken your family. If only I had consulted Mr. Caversham before coming here—"

"It might have happened anyway," he said, pouring a glass of champagne for her and one for himself. "The situation was always explosive. You are aware, of course, that I was not entirely open with you, even at our last meeting. Do you blame me for that?"

"For not telling me Frank Desmond was Hop's father? Since I was already staying in their house, I am thankful you did not. I should not have known how to face either of them, especially Mrs. Desmond."

"That is what I thought."

She now understood why he himself avoided meeting the Frank Desmonds. And why he had been so angry to find her installed at Edenworth.

"If you had told me, I could have left immediately—"

"Yes, but I was afraid that your leaving the neighbourhood might be the very thing to plunge Eliza into a mood of reckless indiscretion. She was not at all anxious to keep the baby three years ago, and of course it was quite impossible that she should, but this recollection has apparently haunted her ever since, poor girl."

He got up to remove Diana's plate, and was trying to

persuade her to eat a slice of roast lamb when the door was flung open and Henry stood on the threshold.

"I beg your pardon, my lord," he said. "I did not know you were entertaining your mistress."

"Don't be stupid, Henry," said Grove. "You must have realised by now that Mrs. Pentland is not my mistress. You jumped to a fairly natural conclusion when you first met her with a little boy who has all the Lambert hall-marks. Now you know the secret of Hop's parentage, and it is high time you acknowledged that we all owe Mrs. Pentland a deep debt of gratitude."

"I am sure *you* do, sir," said the young man insolently.

He came into the middle of the room. He had not attempted to change his clothes or comb his tangled black locks; instead he had been drowning his sorrows, and though he was not drunk there was a febrile glitter in his eyes. He was taller and slighter than his father, and very handsome in a dramatic style. The thought darted through the back of Diana's mind that Henry looked the complete romantic hero, while Grove was much more like an English gentleman.

"Do you mind explaining that last remark?" Grove asked quietly.

"Isn't it plain enough?" retorted Henry. "Mrs. Pentland may not be the child's mother, but what kind of a woman did you choose to share the story of my sister's disgrace? How did this squalid conspiracy come about? I was the person who ought to have been consulted! You were not supposed to have any dealings with Eliza at that time. You got hold of her, no doubt, induced her to deceive my mother—you are to blame for what has happened. My dear little sister so innocent and so pure, you and your friends led her astray, set her a bad example—"

"I know that you have had a great shock," said Grove, now rather white. "All the same, you cannot seriously imagine that I helped to corrupt Eliza!"

"Why not?" said Henry wildly. "A man who lives as you do soon blurs the distinctions of right and wrong. It cannot have troubled you much that she had a bastard child, or why is Frank Desmond still alive? A father who loved his daughter would have killed her seducer. But then you never did care much for either of us. You deserted us when we were hardly out of the nursery."

Henry was possibly too distressed to know what he was saying. Grove understood this, but he was not proof against the last accusation because it echoed his own deep sense of guilt. Diana saw the pain in his face and could no longer remain passive.

"Mr. Lambert, please listen to me!" she said in a clear, determined voice.

Henry glanced at her in surprise.

"Instead of making these random attacks on your father, why don't you try to discover what really happened? You wonder how I came into this business: very well, I'll tell you. I first saw your sister crouching on a London doorstep in an extremity of pain and terror. I took her into my lodgings, where she soon afterwards gave birth to a son. She would not tell me her name, only that she was called Eliza, and that she was not married. I tried to persuade her to get in touch with her friends but she always refused. She told me she lived with her mother and an elder brother to whom she was much attached. I begged her to confide in her brother. This reduced her to a state of utter misery. She cried a great deal and said, 'If he knew what I'd done, he would be so disgusted and mortified he would never speak to me again. I think he would hate me.' I have never forgotten the awful impression those words made on me."

Henry caught his breath but did not speak.

She went on, inexorably. "I was at a loss what to do. My husband was dead and I had been left very badly off. At the end of a fortnight my landlady pointed out to Eliza that we could neither of us support her and her baby indefinitely. This induced her to go and seek out someone she described as the man who was most likely to protect her. She was so much happier when she came back that I assumed she had been to see her lover. After that, Lord Grove took care of everything. It was arranged that I should bring up the baby as my own. In consequence I have received a most generous allowance and his lordship has always taken an interest in Hop, yet he has been so careful of your sister's reputation that I was never told who she was or where she came from. It's a pity you didn't know these things before you started abusing him. He is the only one of you who has done anything to help Eliza. What did you and your mother do? You let her fall in love with Frank Desmond, she became his mistress and you did not know; you never even noticed that she was expecting a child. All that either of you ever achieved was to frighten her so with your high-minded morality that she dared not confide in you and thought it useless to confide in her father. If that is your way of showing family affection, I don't think it is much to be proud of."

It was Grove, not Henry, who intervened, saying gently, "Eliza's mother is hardly to be blamed. I believe she was suffering from a nervous disorder at the time."

"Mr. Lambert was not suffering from anything, was he? Apart from his usual spate of resentment?"

Henry turned on his heel and slammed out of the room.

There was a longish silence after this. Diana took a sip of champagne.

"I beg your pardon, Lord Grove. I ought not to have criticized your wife. But I won't pretend to be sorry for what I said about Henry. He is an insufferable young man and the way he behaves to you is disgraceful."

"You must remember that I have not behaved very well towards him."

Diana wondered, not for the first time, what wild infatuation or dark scandal had driven the Groves to the extreme step of living apart. He had paid for his folly, poor man, whatever it was, and seemed likely to go on paying.

***

The butler at Edenworth asked Diana whether she had dined, and then said, "If you care to step into the saloon, ma'am, I will bring the tea tray directly."

"I'll go straight up to my room, thank you."

As she moved towards the staircase, she was brought up short by various unseemly sounds coming from the floor above. An insistent hammering or banging. A man's voice hoarsely demanding, "Let me in! Let me speak to you!" And fainter, so that the words were lost, a woman's furious scolding.

"Good God, what can possibly be——" Diana recollected herself quickly and swung round towards the saloon. "I think I will take tea after all, Greening, if you please."

She could not reach her own room without passing the Desmonds' bedroom door and at the moment this was clearly unthinkable. The butler, looking mournful but very slightly relieved, ushered in the tray and set it on a rosewood table.

He was followed by Walter Desmond, who said with an assumed cheerfulness, "Now you can preside, ma'am, and do everything that is necessary. We shall be very comfortable."

In fact they were both thoroughly embarrassed and Diana was glad to be occupied in unlocking the caddy and ministering to the teapot. As she handed him his cup, Walter brought himself to ask, "What is going on at Brandham? How is Webb taking this miserable business?"

"I don't know, I never saw him. Mrs. Webb has gone to bed, and Mr. Lambert is naturally blaming his father for everything."

"Poor Grove, I dare say he is partly responsible." Walter shot a curious glance at Diana; like the others, he must now be uncertain of her exact position. "The late Lady Grove always struck me as a stupid woman, her mind was filled with a curious confusion of Evangelical prudery and acute sensibility; I think her son and daughter would both have been better guided by their father. Though it's hardly for me to sit in judgment on the Lamberts, when the villain of the piece is so evidently my own brother. To debauch a girl of sixteen, his wife's cousin, it passes all bounds. I can scarcely believe it, even now."

Diana sipped her tea from the almost transparent porcelain cup. She found it refreshing after the champagne, which had made her thirsty.

"I think I had better make arrangements to leave Edenworth immediately."

"Leave?" he repeated startled. "I hope you won't do any such thing—unless you are afraid of being contaminated by the scandal."

"I hope I'm not so poor spirited. But you cannot have considered, Captain Desmond: my poor little Hop, through no fault of his, can hardly be welcome here now.

Your sister-in-law will not like her children to associate with their father's bastard."

"I don't know whether she'll care about that," he said slowly. "Please don't go unless you feel quite convinced you are unwelcome. They do need a third person—I am expecting to be recalled to the War Office any day now—and I was relying on you to act as a mediator."

It was not an enviable prospect. They sat in silence. Diana was thinking of the raised voices on the upper floor, and she guessed that Walter was thinking of them too, for he got up, saying that he thought one of the dogs was scratching at the door, and opened it slightly. There was no dog there, and they both remained frankly listening. The house was quiet.

Diana stood up. "I am rather tired, so I shall bid you good night."

Walter responded to this with equal reticence. Saying he had some letters to write, he escorted her to the foot of the staircase and lit her candle for her, the traditional courtesy of a gentleman towards a lady at a country house-party.

Diana climbed the stairs and tiptoed along the wide corridor, past the principal bedroom; the lights up here had all been extinguished. She was a few yards further on when a voice behind her whispered, "Mrs. Pentland."

She turned, holding the candlestick at arm's length, and by the thin flare she saw Frank Desmond sitting on the floor outside his wife's door.

He scrambled to his feet.

"Mrs. Pentland, may I talk to you? Please don't refuse me. I'm in such a desperate fix I hardly know what I'm doing; even my brother is too angry to listen to me, and Maria. . . ." He broke off on something like a sob.

"I have had a very trying day," said Diana truthfully. She had no sympathy to spare for Frank Desmond. "If you simply want to make excuses—"

"No, how could I? What excuse is there for what I did? Only I am still so bewildered; that fine little boy of yours, is he really my son? I had no idea of his existence until a few hours ago, and whatever you may think of me, I swear to you I would not have abandoned him—or his mother—if anyone had told me the truth."

"You could not have given his mother the one thing she needed. You were married already."

Even as she said this, Diana realised that Frank probably would have taken care of Hop—he was an extremely affectionate father to his other children—and on this count at least he deserved to have his questions answered.

There was a window at the end of the passage, with a wide windowseat. She sat down there and Frank sat beside her. There was no moon on this dull, damp evening, and she had placed the candle on an oak chest, several feet away. Speaking hardly above a whisper, she told him of Eliza's desperate, pointless visit to her aunt in London, of her panic-stricken wanderings on the day she should have returned home, of her collapse on the doorstep in Sloane Place and everything that followed. She could not see him at all clearly; she sensed enough of his acute distress to be grateful for the darkness.

"If only she had asked me to help her!"

"Would the news have pleased you?"

"Oh, God—you know the answer to that," he said wretchedly.

After a slight pause, as though a spring in his memory had been released, he began to talk of the young people at Brandham as he had first known them.

"I came into this property when I was twenty-one. Having lived only in Ireland or London, and always with crowds of people around me, it was lonely and disconcerting to find myself an English squire in a strange countryside where I didn't know a soul. One of my earliest callers was Henry Lambert. He was eighteen and already used to being treated as the great man of the neighbourhood, since his father was never here. We soon found we had plenty to learn from each other. I returned his call and met his cousin, Maria Cosway. She was enchanting. I fell in love with her on the spot. Henry was in love with her too, and yet at that magic time of our lives we were all three so sincerely attached that there was no room for rivalry or spite. And little Eliza was there in the background. When I say little, she was already taller than Maria, yet very young and unformed in both manners and mind. She must have been about thirteen. It was like having a Newfoundland puppy about the place."

Diana, recalling what Eliza had said, felt the absurd pathos of it all. But how had they drifted into the disastrous love affair?

"Once we were married," Frank continued, "we still saw a great deal of Henry but rather less of Eliza, since she was still in the schoolroom and did not pay visits. I hardly noticed that she was growing up. I was taken up with Maria and our little boy. We were so happy. However, the year after Francis was born we had a great deal of anxiety over Maria's father, who became extremely ill. He took lodgings in Bath, hoping the doctors there could do something for him—a forlorn hope, as we soon realised. Maria was devoted to her father, wanting to be with him continually, and of course I could not refuse to let her go, but I'm afraid I felt a trifle ill-used and very lost without her. I had business here to see to; I could not be forever in Bath. One day I called in at the castle: Henry was away from home and Lady Grove lying down with some nervous ailment. Eliza entertained me and I suddenly realised what a handsome girl she had become. I started a little flirtation: in some ways that was actually worse than what happened later, for there was no need; I did it to amuse myself, because I felt neglected and piqued, and I thought Eliza would be pleased with the attention. I had no idea—talk of putting a spark to dry tinder—and the devil of it was, I found the temptation hard to resist. Still, I knew it was out of the question. I beat a hasty retreat, came home and sat down to dinner in company with the brandy bottle.

"I reckoned without Eliza. She walked along the river bank, the way we went the other night in the boat; it's only about a mile, and she could walk or ride for hours in those days. It was a fine June evening, the long windows were open. She came up through the garden and into the dining room. No one saw her come or go. And I was half drunk. But not too drunk, unfortunately. I'm not trying to excuse myself. The drink didn't prevent my knowing that what I did was wrong—"

"It simply shifted the balance of your judgment, so that the claims of conscience didn't weigh so heavily," suggested Diana, out of her experience of married life in the army.

"Yes." He sounded surprised. "That's exactly what drink does to a man. Well, I rowed Eliza back to Brandham in the boat. She was talking rather wildly and I was beginning to feel every sort of scoundrel. By next morning I was horribly ashamed of myself and had only two thoughts in my head: to run away from Eliza (rather than with her) and to confess the whole dreadful story to Maria and beg her forgiveness. With both these ends in view I set off at once for Bath. When I arrived there I found Maria in despair. Sir Charles Cosway's doctor had ordered some treatment which was doing him more harm than good, and they had engaged a low sort of woman as a nurse, who had been caught stealing. I dealt with these matters, and Maria wept and said how much she depended on me and that she knew I would never fail her. How could I tell her about my wicked folly at such a time? I put it off and put it off and the result was, I never did tell her."

"Were you not afraid that Eliza might have a child?"

"I was in a perpetual state of apprehension for about two months, though I did think it would be confoundedly bad luck—just the one occasion—and when I thought the danger was over I thanked my stars and swore I'd never be unfaithful to Maria again, and I never have been. The idea that Eliza might be able to conceal the birth of a child never crossed my mind. We all know such things have happened, but so rarely that one doesn't consider them. I remained in Bath with Maria until her father died and when we came home Eliza kept out of our way. I believe the next time I saw her was in a London ballroom, and I found her very much changed. Poor girl, I thought I knew the reason for that, and why she's avoided us ever since. I didn't guess the half of it."

Diana reflected that Charley was three months younger than Hop, and that Maria would have written to tell her aunt the good news that she was again pregnant. This must have been the final straw for Eliza. No wonder she had been too proud to appeal to Frank for help. In Sloane Place, after Hop's birth, she had been determined that her own family must never learn the truth. What she had managed to hide even from Diana was the most painful and humiliating part of it: that she had thrown herself at her cousin's husband, who had simply taken her in a moment of self-indulgence, though he was in love with his wife. Probably she had not understood this in the high excitement of her own passion. She must have realised it later.

She had always acted on impulse. Flinging herself into Frank's arms, leaving her aunt's house with nowhere to go, carrying Hop off on that ridiculous odyssey to see the coaches; she was as hopeless a romantic in her own way as her unworldly prig of a brother. Diana remembered what Walter had said about their parents.

"You won't repeat any of this?" Frank was saying. "Not even to Grove?"

"Certainly not to Lord Grove."

"I should never dream of telling any of Eliza's family that she deliberately came here to seek me out, uninvited. If they ask for details, of course I must take the blame. I'm years older than she is and I behaved abominably, flirting with the poor little girl when she was too green to know that it was all make-believe. It was a despicable thing to do. I've told you what really happened, in confidence, because I want to ask your advice: do you think Maria would find it easier to forgive me if she knew? At present she seems to imagine I was in love with Eliza. And she is so angry, she won't let me explain. I don't know what to do."

"Give her time," said Diana. "I expect she would prefer the true version, though I should wait until she has recovered her temper. Otherwise she may refuse to believe it. And Mr. Desmond, don't be offended, but I hope you are not intending to spend the night lying on the passage floor. It won't accomplish anything. Your wife is not a sentimental girl of sixteen."

She heard him draw a sharp breath and felt she had been needlessly unkind.

Then he said, "You are right, of course. Romantic extravagance isn't going to restore my credit as a husband, is it? The trouble is, you see, that I do still love Maria in that way. Only she'll never believe it any more."

III

──

Diana had barely finished dressing next morning, and was still seated at the dressing table, when Maria came to see her.

Diana caught a first glimpse of her, pale and hostile, in the looking-glass, and thought, she has come to turn us out. I thought she would.

Feeling a little sick at the prospect of yet another scene, she said, "I am sure you are anxious to be rid of us, Mrs. Desmond. Will you let me send a message to Brandham? I must ask Lord Grove where he wants us to go."

Ignoring this, and staring her straight in the eye, Maria asked, "Did you know when you came here that Hop was Frank's child?"

"Good heavens, no! I should never have come if I'd had the smallest suspicion. This may seem incredible to you, but when I arrived at Brandham, I did not even know who his mother was. That is to say, I recognised the young woman I had taken into my lodgings in Hans Town, but I had no idea that she was the Honourable Mrs. Webb and I knew nothing of her previous history and family connections."

Maria unbent a good deal after the first few words, and said, "I am very glad to hear you say so. I should have known that you would not be so two-faced. The fact is, I have been dreadfully deceived and I don't know whom to trust."

"Yes, I can imagine that. I am very sorry."

"Then you will not go away and leave me? There is no reason why you should."

Diana hesitated. If Hop's presence in her house did not seem an intolerable hardship to Maria, there was no point in making an issue of it.

"I must have someone I can talk to," pursued Maria.

She certainly had closer women friends than Diana, whom she had met so recently; none of these others was in the secret and any confidences would have to begin with the sordid story of Frank's unfaithfulness. Diana knew everything already, and nothing that was said to her would spread the scandal any further. It might be best for everyone if she remained here as a listener.

They went down to breakfast, where they were joined by Walter, and all sat down at the table in a civilised manner, with Maria in command of the coffee pot. A few minutes later Frank edged his way into the room as unobtrusively as possible. He was haggard from lack of sleep and pathetically unsure of himself.

"Good morning," he said impartially, as though hoping to include them all without drawing attention to the fact that he had not seen his wife since the night before. "The rain's cleared. I've been down to the farm."

Maria drank her coffee and stood up.

"Where are you going?" he asked her.

She turned to Walter. "Will you make it plain to your brother that I don't intend to speak to him, to sit at the same table, or to have anything to do with him? And ask him to stand aside."

"Oh, come, my dear girl," protested Walter, "how long do you mean to keep this up?"

"For as long as I choose. He's got no right to object. He's been deceiving me for the last four years."

"Maria, don't say that," begged Frank. "I deceived you four years ago, it's true, and I'm desperately sorry. I've done nothing since except keep quiet about it."

Maria said nothing. She simply stared him down. Defeated and miserable, he let her pass.

"Who would have thought she could be such a shrew?" muttered Walter. No longer critical of his brother, he was inclined to take his part.

Presently Diana went out into the garden, where she saw a charming procession: a flock of nursemaids in starched caps and aprons, like large white birds, escorting their fledglings across the gravel sweep to the avenue, where there was a swing hanging from a branch of one of the walnut trees. She went to join them.

Hop had completely recovered from yesterday's adventure, and Sukey seemed to have forgotten her terrors. She was the oldest of the children and the only girl (apart from baby Henrietta, carried about in her nurse's arms and too young to compete) so she enjoyed ordering the boys about, even though they did not take much notice. Diana played with them and Nancy gave them turns on the swing. It was strange to think that these little boys were Hop's half-brothers; Diana could not see any resemblance, for the Lambert strain was so strong, but it did strike her that Hop's beguiling ways had probably come from his father—the irresistible gift of Irish charm.

Frank came out and stood watching them from a distance: his three sons; Diana thought he was paying particular attention to the unacknowledged son who tumbled about so merrily with Francis and Charley. Once Frank made as if to come and join them. Then he glanced back at the windows of the house and changed his mind. Afraid to do anything that might increase Maria's anger.

"Why doesn't Papa come and play?" asked Francis.

"You leave your papa alone today," said the nurse. "He has enough on his mind."

Apart from the children, everyone at Edenworth knew what was wrong.

The whole atmosphere had changed. It was a beautiful day, pleasantly cool after the rain, yet the glory of the house and garden, the ordered calm of the sunny rooms, the lovely green serenity, had departed. Diana remembered her first days here, the evening on the river, the party in the hayfield. She had felt that this was a magic place. All her pictures of Edenworth were like bright beads strung together on a thread which was the happy, confident love that united Frank and Maria. Now the thread was broken and the beads had all rolled away.

Maria had retired to her dressing room; she sent a message asking Diana to come and sit with her, and then proceeded to pour out a catalogue of grievances: Frank had betrayed her, he was an adulterer and a liar, she could never respect or trust him again, and she began to find fault with everything concerning him and their life together. He was careless, he was lazy, he was too easy-going with the children, he had been abominably foxed last Christmas at the Brandham Assembly, he spent money like water. And he buried her down here in the provinces; everyone else in their set had a house in town. . . . A week ago she had been claiming that she was never so happy as when they were alone at Edenworth.

And always there was the same refrain, bitter and implacable: "I'll never forgive him. Never as long as I live."

"You think so today, because the shock has been so

great. The pain will grow less, and then I dare say you will not want to quarrel with him any more."

"Yes, I shall. You don't know what it's like. Was your husband ever unfaithful?"

"I'm not sure," said Diana honestly. (There had been a strikingly pretty and disreputable young female at Colchester when the regiment was stationed there. She had not questioned Oliver too closely about this episode.)

Maria considered her very lax.

"Some people can endure any kind of makeshift," she said disdainfully. "I have always held that perfect loyalty and truth should exist between husband and wife, and I look on that as my right. Why should I accept anything less?"

She is spoilt, thought Diana, surprised at the discovery. It was the last epithet she would once have applied to Maria, so generous and sweet-tempered in her family life, so free from pride or affectation, so considerate to her servants and dependents: the very model of what a privileged young woman ought to be. Maria had found it easy to be good because she was happy, and superficially her happiness had nothing to do with money or position, but of course it was her great wealth which had made life so smooth for her. She had never encountered the worries and disappointments of a soldier's wife in wartime: the frequent moves, wretched billets, endless economies, above all the constant fear of impending separation. Diana had learnt fortitude in a hard school. She regarded Maria with a curious mixture of pity and envy.

A luncheon tray was brought up to them in the dressing room, and afterwards Diana suggested they should take a stroll in the garden.

"Do come. The air will do you good."

"I don't want to be done good, I feel too low. You go—I'd just as soon be left alone."

She was determined to make the worst of things.

In the corridor Diana met Watson, Maria's maid. They exchanged glances of uncomfortable complicity, and she would have passed on when the older woman stopped her.

"Excuse me, ma'am, for mentioning it, but I hope you will try to persuade my mistress not to be too hard on Mr. Desmond."

Diana would have expected a staid, middle-aged lady's maid to take the wife's part against the husband in this kind of domestic fracas. Was Watson susceptible to Irish charm? She looked too sensible to let it sway her judgment.

"Mrs. Desmond's feelings have been very much hurt," Diana reminded her. "Whatever she is saying today, I am sure she will soon become more moderate."

"That's just it, ma'am—I'm afraid she may not. To hear her talk, I can't help being reminded of her ladyship."

"Of Mrs. Desmond's mother?"

"Oh no, ma'am, I never saw Lady Cosway. I was speaking of the Viscountess. The late Lady Grove. I come from Brandham, ma'am; all my family was in service at the castle, and the way her ladyship used to carry on you would not credit. Mind you, I don't say his lordship was everything that a husband should be, very few gentlemen are. Still, he *is* a gentleman and always behaved as such in his own home, and she nagged him night and day, gave him no peace. Everyone was against him when he took and left her, saying he'd behaved so disgracefully, but we servants knew what he'd had to put up with. And I shouldn't like to think of my young lady taking after her aunt. She grew up at the castle, you know, and I dare say she heard things she wasn't meant to."

She went downstairs and into the garden, abandoning the Desmonds' troubles for a while as she thought about the Groves. So here was the answer, the cause of the separation. Not some hideous scandal, too shocking to mention. Just the fact that Grove could not stand his wife's nagging. It was probably this, rather than his love affairs, which now made him feel guilty, for if Watson was right he was no worse than a great many other husbands and had done nothing which would give his wife a moral claim to live apart from him. He had not been cruel or vicious. He had simply deserted his family because he was not prepared to listen to the sort of complaints that Maria had been airing all the morning about Frank. And who should blame him? Unfortunately he had left his children as well as his wife, so now he was blaming himself for what she had made of them.

Diana had not noticed where she was going, and found herself walking in the green bowling-alley between the dense yew hedges, where she had walked with Grove on Monday. The turf was fresh and brilliant after the rain. Although she was not thinking much about her surroundings, she presently got the idea that there was someone on the other side of the outer hedge, the one nearest to the river. It was impossible to see anything between the tight branches of almost black leaves, but she could hear this person keeping pace with her, stopping when she stopped, only not quite quickly enough. Who could it be? She did not like the sensation of being spied on. Walking noisily and humming a tune, she stumped along till she was about three feet from the end of the hedge, stood quite silent for a moment, and then darted round the corner.

She came face to face with Horace Webb.

They stared at each other in astonishment, but while she was indignant, he looked decidedly sheepish.

"Mr. Webb—what are you doing, skulking here in this furtive manner?"

"I beg your pardon, Mrs. Pentland. I—I did not mean to alarm you."

"I am not alarmed, though I should like to know what

you mean by it." Diana was seized with the absurd notion that he had come slinking over to Edenworth like a villain in a melodrama, to murder Frank Desmond. He did not really look the part; he was unarmed and wore a rather townish grey coat, a high cravat, and a general air of fashion which was somehow a little pathetic, considering his disconsolate expression.

"I left my groom in the lane—I didn't go to the house —I'm still not sure what I should do. I was trying to make up my mind. My brother-in-law says I am in honour bound to call Desmond out."

"He would!" said Diana.

Among all the other unpleasant prospects, she had not thought of the possibility of a duel between Eliza's husband and her seducer. She now saw that this was exactly what Henry Lambert would consider essential, no matter how little it achieved or how many innocent people were hurt.

"I can see you don't approve, ma'am. Ladies seldom do. Only it isn't easy to know—I was brought up to think duelling was wrong, and if I was a better shot than Desmond none of those high-and-mighty Lamberts could call me a coward for refusing to fight him. As it is, I'm no match for a fellow like that, I could never hit him by design, and Eliza's family know it. They despise me because my grandfather was a buttonmaker."

"Well, I can see no reason why you should risk getting yourself killed, if it is only to score off your wife's relations," remarked Diana, not without a touch of contempt.

He looked at her with so much pain in his eyes that she was startled. "Do you think it is any pleasure to me to be alive at present?"

"I suppose not. I beg your pardon."

"If one could just die and be out of the way—it is the thought of a duel that is so tormenting. For although I may not be able to shoot Desmond deliberately, and I daresay he would not want to shoot me, in the circumstances, the fact is that once you get two men with loaded pistols, anything may happen. And think of the effect on Eliza if one of us was killed. Even where there isn't a spark of affection, I doubt if any woman can feel her honour has been avenged or her conscience cleared because one man has been forced into slaughtering another on her account. I think it must make everything worse, quite apart from the scandal."

"I entirely agree." She was struck by the perception in this speech, and said, "You are anxious to avoid distressing her?"

"Of course. I am—attached to her, whatever she has done. I dare say you had not realised that?"

"I was not sure."

Then it all came out. He had been drawn to Eliza the first time he saw her in a London drawing room, so tall and silent among all the silly chatterboxes. He decided she was very shy, and this had increased his sympathy towards her, for he was shy himself. She listened with apparent pleasure when he talked about steam-engines and other unusual topics, and her brother had encouraged him, saying that Eliza liked him better than all their other acquaintance, and that she was a different creature in a close family circle among people she knew well. And she had been different, Horace commented grimly, for as soon as they were married she made it plain that she hated the sight of him.

"God knows why she accepted me. If it's true that she wants a child to replace the one she was obliged to part with, then she's going a deuced odd way about it, for she can't bear me to touch her."

"Are you saying that she won't let you—that you have never—"

"Not since the first two months," mumbled Horace, red in the face and staring at his boots. "She never refused.

She was compliant. Obedient. And I didn't want that: it was horrible, to feel her go rigid with distaste and to hear her crying in the night. I couldn't stand it."

"I suppose she was afraid of your discovering her secret, poor girl."

His head jerked up. "I never thought of that!"

"How should you? Until yesterday you did not know she had a secret to hide. Yet she must have suffered a great degree of anxiety and remorse."

Eliza, having lost her nerve, had probably imagined that her bridegroom was a man of the world who would soon realise that he had been tricked. In spite of everything, she was still so innocent that she did not allow for Horace's inexperience and diffidence, his total inability to deal with a reluctant wife. Shut up like hermits in their separate cells of loneliness and hurt pride, they had spent two miserable years, and it was only too natural that Eliza should have begun to brood more and more over her lost baby.

"Have you seen your wife since all this business came out?" Diana asked the now abstracted Horace Webb.

He shook his head. "She is in bed and sees no one. You don't know what things are like at Brandham. Henry is so angry with me for being a poltroon that I can't get a civil word out of him. He and his father are not on speaking terms, and Lord Grove never notices me anyway. The only person one can talk to is Ledbury."

Diana spared a thought for poor Lord Ledbury, playing a similar part to her own, which seemed to be that of a confidante going mad in white linen.

She said, "I think you should try and talk to your father-in-law."

"I don't know what good that will be. I can never be in his company without making a fool of myself. He holds me in the greatest contempt; he did his best to prevent my marrying his daughter because I was not grand enough for them——at least I suppose that was the reason," added Horace, suddenly aware of different possibilities.

"Lord Grove was very awkwardly placed. He was the only member of her family who knew there was a reason why you might not wish to marry her. I dare say he feels you have cause to reproach him."

"Reproach Grove? I shouldn't dare!" said Horace frankly.

She could not help smiling. "I have just realised that he is the one person who can solve your dilemma over the duel. All this wretched business happened before you ever met Eliza Lambert; she was an unmarried girl and the proper person to defend her honour was her father. If he did not choose to fight Frank Desmond then, I expect he will agree with you that there is no virtue in your fighting him now. I think you ought at least to consult him."

Horace was so struck by this argument that he felt he really must manage to ask for an interview with his father-in-law. Having thanked Diana repeatedly for her advice, he hurried away from Edenworth, unseen by any of the Desmonds. She went back to the house, glad to perceive a ray of light in all the gloom——Horace at least was not out for vengeance, and perhaps this upheaval might actually lead to a better understanding between him and Eliza. Then she began to have qualms. Horace seemed to find Grove so intimidating, it would be a pity if they succeeded in rubbing each other up the wrong way, as they always had before.

There was a writing table in the small saloon. She sat down and wrote a brief note to Grove, giving the gist of her conversation with Horace, and begging him not to snub the young man, whose disposition was so much better than his manner. Horace, she reflected, was showing up much more favourably than Maria, the other injured party.

She rang for the butler and asked him, with a good deal

of suppressed embarrassment, to have her note sent to the Castle. Greening, quite impassive, said he would do so immediately.

Three hours later she received a reply, addressed in the well-known hand she associated with Mr. Wood, and sealed with an imposing crest.

> Brandham Castle.
> 5th July.

My dear Mrs. Pentland,

Once again I am in your debt. H. Webb demanded an audience—that is how it sounded—and I believe we should have come to a deadlock but for your timely warning. Having made strenuous endeavours not to appear as an ogre, I found him a great deal more sensible and conciliating than I ever did before. He seems truly anxious to do all he can for my poor Eliza, and to live with her again if she agrees, which is more than we have any right to expect. I have prevailed on her to see him, and he is with her now; far more usefully employed than he would have been fighting Desmond. Not that I blame him for his indecision—no young man likes to be thought a coward—but what a piece of folly!

Henry is in a passion, as you may suppose, and insists on playing Laertes as though he was Hamlet.

I hope to call on you very soon, there are some serious matters I should like to discuss. I cannot find words to express my gratitude for your constant kindness to so many members of my family. God bless you.

> Grove.

IV

On Friday morning Diana spent some time in the garden with Sukey, Hop, and Nancy, thankful to escape from the atmosphere indoors. During their walk they were obliged to call in at the stables, so that Hop could admire the horses in their stalls, and there on the cobbles, in the shade of the coach house, Diana saw the Brandham Castle landau.

So there were visitors from the castle. One visitor presumably, for neither Henry nor the Webbs were likely to call here at present. It would be most unlucky Diana thought for her to be out here if he—if anyone wished to see her. Making a slight excuse, she left the children with Nancy and returned to the house. She knew she was being disingenuous, and felt slightly ashamed of herself. However sincerely he expressed his gratitude, Grove could not really need to consult her.

The hall was deserted. She was disappointed, uncertain

what to do. One could not go hunting for someone who might be engaged in a private conversation. Nor loiter here, to be noticed by the servants. Much to her relief, Walter Desmond appeared from the direction of the library.

"Mrs. Pentland, may I have a word with you?" He took her into the blue saloon. "Did you know Henry was here?"

"Henry? No. I saw the landau and I thought—" So much for her own silly manoeuvrings. She pulled herself together. "What does he want?"

"Frank's blood. What else? Henry has called him out and of course Frank can't refuse."

She listened in dismay. Henry had jeered at his father for allowing Frank to live; he had done his best to shame Horace into fighting. This was the logical sequel.

"He'll kill Frank," said Walter gloomily.

"Is not your brother a very good shot?"

"You don't understand. Frank means to delope. Fire into the air. He has told me so."

Diana knew that a duellist sometimes did this when he felt he was in the wrong. And of course Frank Desmond was in the wrong. His selfish weakness had caused a great deal of misery, but his death would cause a great deal more.

"Can't it be stopped?" she said.

"I'm afraid not. They are both determined to get it over at once, this morning. That's all wrong—one is supposed to wait for tempers to cool—only Frank wants me as his second, and it's better than dragging in an outsider. Henry's brought Ledbury to act for him, and a surgeon."

"If you refused to act as their seconds—"

"I should like to, but Frank has begged me to stand by him, and I must. I did have one last hope. I thought that if Maria was willing to intercede with Henry, he might withdraw. He has always been devoted to her."

From his tone, Diana knew that Walter had already tried Maria and failed.

"I suppose she will not intervene?"

"She says she does not care what happens to Frank. How any woman could be so—well, I mustn't speak my mind on that subject. I wanted to tell you, Mrs. Pentland, only to prepare you for something very unpleasant within the next hour. We can rely on you not to lose your head."

Diana hoped he was right. She felt dreadfully inadequate, left alone in the blue saloon with nothing to do but wait. Was it really too late to avert disaster? Perhaps if she went at once to Maria she could somehow pierce the wall of callous and unforgiving indifference and persuade her to act before it was too late.

As she stood there wondering, Diana saw an ominous little group skirting the parterre outside. There were five purposeful backs: the Desmond brothers leading the way, then a burly man who must be the surgeon. Then Henry and Lord Ledbury.

She opened the window and stepped out on to the terrace. She saw the grim little procession turn in between the yew hedges and began to follow. She knew she ought not to do this. She could not prevent the duel and women were quite excluded from so-called affairs of honour. Oliver would have been horrified. She did not care. At the entrance to the bowling alley she paused, expecting to find the combatants in battle array, but the long green enclosure was empty, which surprised her. Surely this was private enough for them? Then she realised that the alley ran north and south, so that one of the marksmen would have been firing into the sun. This would not do; the semblance of British fair play had to be observed.

She hurried over the shorn grass till she came to an opening in the hedge and looked down a narrow vista towards the river. Stone urns and mossy steps, running between trees and bushes. And not a soul in sight. She stood for a moment to get her breath, and heard a faint sound, perhaps the snapping of a branch, somewhere down there on the right.

Then much closer, just behind her, a man running.

"Which way did they go?" demanded Grove.

"Over to the right I think." She looked at him with renewed hope. His active, positive presence made her feel that the situation might still be saved. "How did you know?"

"Horace told me," said Grove, striding past her. "Go back to the house, Diana. This is not fit for you."

Diana noted with an odd, distant pleasure that he had used her Christian name; she paid no further attention but followed him down the steps. A pathway led off to the right through a little hazel copse, and beyond this, on a natural stage of even turf overlooking the river, was a spectacle that chilled her to the heart—it was so stark, so formal, so filled with deadly implications.

Henry and Frank faced each other across an open space, erect and still. Each gripped an identical duelling pistol. The seconds stood to one side, Ledbury had a white handkerchief ready to give the signal. The surgeon was carefully looking the other way.

"Stop!" shouted Grove.

The five men shifted and the image dissolved.

"Thank God you are here, my lord," said the surgeon, with obvious relief. "This is a sorry business."

"Then what are you about, Redmayne, to lend it countenance? I thought better of you."

"Had I refused to come, they would have managed without me."

"I dare say." Grove glanced at Walter and Ledbury. "And no doubt you are both here under the same dispensation?"

Ledbury began to speak, but was interrupted by Henry who broke out furiously, "You have no right to stop us, my lord. Since you've shirked your duty in this manner, it has nothing to do with you."

"Yes it has," retorted his father. "It is the duty of every law-abiding citizen to prevent a breach of the peace. I could summon a magistrate and have you committed, the whole lot of you, and at this moment nothing would give me greater pleasure. Desmond, you may let me have that lethal instrument."

Frank complied at once, handling the weapon with great care, and saying, "It would not have been lethal in this case. Please believe me, my lord—I had no intention of hitting him. I've done enough harm already."

"I guessed as much." Grove turned towards Henry. "Do I have to explain to you that your notions about your own honourable and gallant conduct are completely deluded? You know, or at least you should know, that a man of Desmond's upbringing does not shoot to wound or kill when he knows he is entirely in the wrong. Especially if his opponent is an old friend and a family connection. This was not a meeting between gentlemen that you forced on him. It would have been a firing-party, with you as the self-appointed executioner. Well, I don't care to have my son exacting vengeance like a Corsican brigand. Give me that pistol."

Diana had never heard him speak in this tone before, and she was almost sorry for Henry. He was so humiliated and so furious (partly, perhaps, with himself) that he could not bear even to bring the pistol to his father. Instead he threw it on the ground in a gesture of childish temper.

There was a flash and a crack and at the same instant Frank cried a warning and flung himself forward, knocking Grove nearly off his feet. As Grove staggered back and recovered his balance, Frank himself went down, with a bright red gash spurting across his thigh.

Diana heard herself scream out as she ran forward, colliding with the surgeon, who was trying to open his case of instruments.

"Hold this," he said, thrusting the case at her. "Not afraid of blood, are you?"

"No, no! But do hurry."

There was blood everywhere: on Frank's clothes, spreading in a great stain; on Grove's hands, as he knelt beside the wounded man, trying to staunch the flow from the severed artery; blood splashed around on the grass.

She unrolled bandages and gave Redmayne the things he asked for. Beyond Grove's shoulder she could see Walter supporting his brother in his arms. Frank's face was the colour of wax.

"Tell Maria—" he said. "Tell Maria—"

There was a sharp smell of singeing in the air, and the squawk of birds disturbed by the shot. And Henry's dazed voice saying, "I didn't mean it to go off. I never thought."

"You never do think," said Grove, without looking up.

Redmayne got his tourniquet firmly fixed in place. Meanwhile, Ledbury had taken Henry with him to fetch the door of the boathouse, which they removed from its hinges to act as a stretcher. It was very heavy, and so was the patient, who was now unconscious, either from pain or loss of blood, and it needed the strength of four men to carry him back to the house with Mr. Redmayne walking beside Frank to make sure he was not unduly jolted. Diana walked on the other side, watching to see that Walter's coat remained in the right position as a pillow. It was an anxious and difficult journey and no one was disposed to talk.

As they drew near the house, emerging from the shelter of the yew hedges, Grove said, "Perhaps you would go ahead and warn them, Mrs. Pentland."

She was about to do so, when they saw a slim figure in white standing at the edge of the geometric parterre, staring down towards the river. She waited long enough to recognise the walking figures and then came running towards them in a state of wild distraction.

"Frank?" she called out. "He's not badly hurt? Oh God!" She was now near enough to see the recumbent figure. "He's not dead?"

"He's lost a lot of blood, ma'am, that's all," said Redmayne. "It's a flesh wound; no damage to the bone, I believe."

Maria did not seem to hear him. She was weeping silently as she gazed down at her husband's shuttered face.

"My dearest boy," she whispered. "My dear love. How could I have been so cruel? It's all my fault—only I did not think you would really shoot him, Henry."

"I wasn't aiming at him," said the luckless Henry. "There was no duel, this was an accident."

"An accident?"

"As far as Frank was concerned," said Grove. "In fact he most heroically put himself in the way and saved my life. Henry would much rather have hit me."

Frank was carried upstairs and put to bed by Maria and Watson, assisted by his valet and supervised by Mr. Redmayne. Maria's remorse was not the stupid, sentimental kind which would have made her useless in a sickroom; she rallied all her natural good sense for the task of nursing her husband, and as Watson was also an experienced nurse Diana soon decided she was not necessary to them. She went downstairs again with a vague idea of looking for the nursery party who had gone for their usual airing; it would not do for them to be frightened by exaggerated stories.

As she passed the breakfast room, an anxious voice asked, "How is he going on, Mrs. Pentland? Is there any change?"

"The surgeon seems quite satisfied."

Henry was looking so dejected that she did not like to go away and leave him. He was seated at the table, lean-

ing on his elbows. The dark lock fell forward over his
brow, and that shortened finger was very noticeable.

"How could I have been such a fool?" he said with a
sort of groan. "Throwing down a loaded pistol, it was the
act of a lunatic. I ought to have known—of course I did
know. I had been so eager to settle with Frank for ruining
my sister—and now I'm in his debt. If he hadn't been so
prompt, my father would have been hit in the stomach.
He thinks I wanted to kill him."

"He said that in a moment of stress."

"He might have been dead by now, and I should never
have been able to say—"

"To say what, Mr. Lambert?"

"I don't know. Except that I never can say anything to
him now that is not hostile and ungracious. It was not always so. When I was a boy, before he went away, we
used to have such fine times. He was the best of fathers."

Diana had a sudden vivid memory of Grove on the
common at Great Wickfield, showing Hop how to fly a
kite, and of his change of mood, the sadness in his expression, when she asked about his own children. Hop
(though she could not have guessed this at the time) must
have been the image of the little boy he had once loved.

"I resented his going," continued Henry in a low voice,
"so I made up my mind to hate him, and the truth is, I
became horribly jealous. I see that now."

"Jealous of Lord Grove?"

"Everyone thinks the world of him, haven't you noticed? His friends and his neighbours at Paraden, and his
tenants—yes, and his tenants at Brandham, too. He
hasn't been up here for eleven years, not since he left my
mother, and I've done my best to take his place, but directly his lordship comes on the scene, everyone is flock-
ing round him again. And Eliza—I never could make out
why she wanted to write to him and visit him as soon as
she was old enough—and now I learn that they had this

secret between them; that when she was in such great trouble she turned to him instead of me. Poor girl, I would have helped her gladly; how could she think otherwise? I suppose that's why I was so mad to punish Frank —it seemed the only thing my father had left undone. I was too stupid to grasp the point: that Frank's a good fellow at heart and he was bound to delope. I've made a hash of everything and naturally my father despises me.

"Mind you, he's always done that. I'm a disappointment to him. He'd have preferred a son like Walter, someone who joined the army and served on Lord Wellington's staff, not a fool who wastes his time restoring Gothic ruins. He thinks I'm affected and conceited, and I know I've behaved badly to him, but he need not talk as though I'm simply waiting to step into his shoes. He's forever doing it, and after what happened this morning—"

Henry broke off. Diana thought he was on the verge of tears. She realised that this was jealousy of a different kind, not resentment at his father's popularity, which sounded merely petty, but something more fundamental: a desperate need for his father's approval. She also realised that she had left the door very slightly ajar and that a man's shadow ran in a dark line down the gap. She wondered how long he had been there.

The shadow vanished; then there were footsteps, the rattle of the handle, all the noise of an arrival, and Grove came in, saying, "Ah, there you both are! Redmayne and I have been selecting a plausible accident. It appears that we were out shooting rabbits when Frank stumbled and his gun went off. It will have to be rabbits because it's too early for partridges."

Henry got up and went over to the window. With his back to them, he said: "It seems rather hard that Frank should bear the stigma of being so infernally careless. Don't you think I was the one to fall over my gun, sir? It would be more in character."

Grove exchanged a rueful glance with Diana.

"Not according to Redmayne," he said bracingly. "He has been singing your praises for the last half-hour. He says that fathers never know when they are in luck, and he sees a good deal of family life, so I daresay he is right. As for that business with the pistol, don't blame yourself too much; there was some excuse. I did goad you. But then I'd had a bad fright, and that always affects one's temper."

"What sort of a fright?" asked Henry innocently.

"My dear boy, do you suppose I am entirely indifferent to your fate?"

Henry turned round. "Oh well, I didn't think—that is—you had already guessed that Frank wouldn't hurt me."

"There are worse disasters than being shot. I could not help imagining how you might feel after you'd shot him. How do you feel towards him now, by the way? Do you still hate him as much as you did two hours ago?"

"No," said Henry slowly. "When I saw him lying there on the ground, the hatred melted away. Which is quite illogical, for what he did to Eliza is still just as monstrous. Nothing can change that."

"No, but humanity is stronger than reason: one is purged by pity and terror. It must take a very coldblooded man to kill an old friend and live comfortably with the recollection." Grove smiled slightly. "I don't think either you or I would pass the test."

This apparently started a new train of thought.

"Did you ever want to fight Frank, sir?"

"I wanted to break his neck," said Grove, and he sounded as though he meant it literally. "But since I was aware of all the objections, it would have been some satisfaction to confront him with the truth and force him to recognise the harm he had done. I felt it was iniquitous that he should go on living in untroubled bliss without a shred of remorse, as far as I could see. Only I dared not risk my confrontation. Once he heard about the child, I thought he might very likely plunge into action: try to approach Eliza or confess the whole thing to Maria—and once Maria knew, the whole family would be bound to hear. That was the very thing Eliza had begged me to avoid. My chief aim was to protect her, and there were other people to consider: you and your mother, Maria herself—and I knew how much misery she and her children might be spared if she never found out. So I kept my mouth shut.

"Though I was never quite magnanimous enough to enjoy the sight of Frank's domestic bliss. In fact I couldn't endure it. That's the real reason I've never been back to Brandham since your mother died: I didn't want to meet Frank and Maria. Yet who am I to judge Frank Desmond? After the havoc of the last few days, I don't even wish to. I just feel sorry for the poor devil."

Henry was gazing at Grove as though he had never seen him before, never believed him capable of such thoughts and feelings. Was he also adding to his father's stature and elevating his sentiments to fit the landscape of his own imagination? Diana decided that this was unfair. Henry might be romantic but he was not basically stupid, and once he was prepared to learn from his father, he would soon develop a sense of proportion.

In the meantime they would have to be patient with each other. They had plenty to talk about. She remembered the errand that had brought her downstairs, and went quietly to find the children.

V

During the next three days Maria hardly left her husband's bedside. Both Diana and Watson frequently offered to take her place for an hour or two, but she could
not bear to leave him. From the moment he first opened
his eyes and remembered the immediate past, Frank must
have known that all was forgiven, for Maria was smiling
down at him, and after that Diana often found them
holding hands.

By Monday the wound was healing so well that Maria
was willing to leave him while he had an afternoon sleep,
and to sit with Diana in the blue saloon. Walter had driv-
en back to London on Saturday.

"I don't know what happened to me last week," admitted Maria, as she tidied some reels of silk in the fitted
compartments of her work-table. "I think I must have
been almost mad. Have you ever woken in the night with
an attack of cramp? You know you must not stretch the

muscles of your leg or the pain will become intolerable, yet at the moment of waking you cannot stop yourself. That is how I felt when I was abusing poor Frank and making those scenes. I am ashamed to think how badly I behaved."

"You were very unhappy."

Maria had never mentioned her aunt, and Diana wondered whether she was conscious that her attitude to her husband's infidelity had followed Lady Grove's pattern. It was lucky for the Desmonds that Henry's pistol had gone off before the pattern was set irrevocably in a permanent mould.

Maria sighed. "I suppose it was silly of me to care so much. At the beginning, you know, my mind was so confused that I believed all sorts of dreadful things: I thought Frank and Eliza had been meeting all the time and seeing their baby—I could not listen to his protestations. Now, of course, I understand. What a blessing it has been for them all, your being able to adopt that little boy."

"It has been a blessing for me, too."

"Yes." Maria fiddled with her embroidery scissors. "You have given him your name and let everyone think he is your son. I suppose it is possible that you may find it a trifle awkward—that you might wish—in short, Frank and I have been talking it over, and if at any time the arrangement became an obstacle, we should be very glad to have dear little Hop here and bring him up with Charley and the others. I should love him like a son, I promise you."

Diana was astonished and annoyed. "Of course I shall never wish to part with Hop! He has become as much my own child as Sukey. I am sure you mean to be kind, but it's out of the question."

She must have sounded quite fierce, for Maria said, "Please do not be offended, dear Diana."

And at that moment the butler announced Lord Grove.

"We've come to visit the sick," said Grove, shaking hands with them both. "Henry will be here in a minute; he's taken the curricle round to the yard. He's hoping to see Frank for a short time, if that is allowed. I can come back another day; I daresay two of us would be excessive."

"I expect he would like to see you both, Uncle Harry, if you don't mind waiting. He is asleep at present."

So Grove's name was Henry too. Diana had not realised that, though Mr. Wood, she now remembered, had signed with the initial H. And it occurred to her now that Eliza had called the baby after her father, not her brother. She heard Maria asking rather stiffly for news of Eliza.

"She is a great deal better, I'm glad to say. Horace is taking her for a tour of the Welsh mountains; his own idea, and she seems quite excited at the prospect. Horace has some very good qualities, once you get to know him, and he is certainly fond of Eliza. Naturally they would not come to Edenworth, knowing how you must feel at present, though I hope there won't be a lasting break. She has written to you, Maria: it was a penitential exercise, so read it with what charity you can."

He drew a letter from his pocket, adding, "I have one for you also, Mrs. Pentland." Though he did not produce this.

Maria turned the letter over and over in her hands. Then she seemed to collect herself, and said, "I'll just go and meet Henry; Frank may be awake by now. Mrs. Pentland will entertain you, sir."

She hurried out of the room.

"That will be delightful," murmured Grove, sitting back in his chair and surveying Diana with his intensely blue gaze. "I haven't seen you since the great affray. You were kind to Henry that morning."

"All I did was to listen. He is very much attached to you, even if he doesn't care to show it."

"That's often the way with families, isn't it? The past has always loomed between us, my differences with his mother, and then we are very unlike in disposition. I know I've sometimes been unjust. For instance, Eliza and I were both wrong in thinking he'd turn against her; he was appalled but he is determined not to let her see it, and to be as affectionate as ever. I can respect him for that."

"So you have not told him to stop playing Laertes as though he was Hamlet?"

She had treasured that remark, while realising that most people would consider it frivolous, if not downright callous. Perhaps one needed Grove's own brand of unsentimental honesty to appreciate that he was neither of these things.

He smiled slightly. "The boy's very young for his age, that's his real trouble. The circumstances that might have brought him on—serious tastes, the care of an independent estate—have probably held him back. Which seems odd to me, but then I was married at nineteen."

"At nineteen?" she repeated. Forced to fulfill a family arrangement, no doubt. What a stupid way to treat a high-spirited young man. It was not surprising he had kicked over the traces. She wondered how old he was now.

"I'm forty-four," said Grove helpfully.

Diana blushed. "It's no concern of mine, my lord—"

"Did you think I was older? I was a practised rake while you were still in the nursery, I'm sure you have grasped that. It's no good trying to look prim, I know there are plenty of stories. Come, what is the worst thing you ever heard about me?"

"That you were an intimate friend of the Regent," said Diana, without pausing to consider.

Grove began to laugh.

"Oh dear, I should not have said that. It sounds so very impertinent. And—and unpatriotic."

He laughed more than ever. "What strange notions you have of patriotism. As a matter of fact, I haven't spoken a civil word to the fellow for years. One can't set much value on a friend who is invariably disloyal to everyone around him. But I own I was dazzled by Prince Florizel when I was young. The life I led then would hardly bear the scrutiny of a gentleman like Mr. Roger Brownlees."

"What on earth has it got to do with Roger Brownlees?" asked Diana, astonished by the intrusion of someone who was no longer important to her, and making this rather plainer than she would have wished.

"It was on his account that you came to Brandham."

That was true. She had been in such a hurry to get away from Great Wickfield that she had forgotten to consult the Noble Client's attorneys, and that was how she had stirred up the hornets' nest. But she had not come away to make up her mind about marrying Brownlees, as she pretended to herself at the time. She had come to escape the embarrassment of his courtship. Because she had known, by the time Mr. Wood had been half an hour at Palfreys, that the worthy Essex squire was not at all the kind of husband she wanted.

Grove got up and stood with one foot on the edge of the fender, one hand in the pocket of his elegant fawn-coloured coat. He had a keen, strong face and the natural poise of a man who was in complete command of all his senses. Whatever his past raking amounted to, he had not allowed it to dull his mind or body.

A silence spread between them. The small saloon, with its deep blue walls, its white plaster swags of fruit and flowers, had become oppressively hot, too overcharged with half-suppressed feelings for so artificial a place. She could neither go on looking at Grove nor look away. They were violently in love and they both knew it.

She had become certain of the symptoms while they were too involved with Eliza's troubles to attend to anything else. And she could not avoid the growing conviction that he wanted to marry her. From the terms they were on, the scrupulous way he had always behaved to her, the many things he had said to her lately, she could not imagine that he would want or expect anything else. Although such an offer would once have been beyond her wildest dreams, it would be absurd and hypocritical to pretend she was not hoping for it.

Only why did he stand there, apparently struck dumb? Surely a man of his assurance couldn't be suffering from diffidence?

Unless—a horrid thought assailed her—unless it wasn't going to be an offer of marriage after all. Was the wealthy aristocrat, with his ancient name and great estates, too proud, when it came to the point, to marry a provincial architect's daughter, the widow of an obscure army officer? If Grove simply wanted her to become his mistress, she did not wish to hear him say so. That declaration would cheapen him more than it cheapened her.

"I—I believe you have a letter for me," she said, almost at random.

"Yes," he agreed, without moving.

"Then may I have it, my lord?"

"I think I had better tell you what it contains. Eliza and Horace want you to know that there will always be a place for Hop in their home, if ever you were to consider parting with him. They propose to pass him off as a distant cousin, and they think his arrival would seem quite natural, since they have no family of their own—though I must say, now their marriage is on a much better footing, I am expecting a tribe of little Webbs in due course."

Diana was no longer listening. Her nerves were already on edge, and she burst out angrily, "I think you are all monsters! So long as Hop's existence was a shameful in-

convenience, you were only too anxious for me to keep
him out of sight. Now that everyone's guilt has been ab-
solved, the poor little innocent is to be snatched away
from the only home he knows and shuttled about between
his mother and father—to gratify their tender con-
sciences, I suppose. If they had any real affection for him
they would not seem to be so selfish."

"You are mistaken," said Grove, when he was able to
interrupt this tirade. "I didn't know the Desmonds had
also offered to take Hop, but it's clear that Maria has
reached the same conclusion as Eliza. They have noticed
that I am in love with you, and I am quite sure you have
noticed it, too, so there's no point in beating about the
bush. And perhaps they are a step ahead of you in realising what people will say if I marry a widow with a three-
year-old child who is the living image of my legitimate
son."

Diana gazed at him with sudden painful comprehen-
sion. He had spoken of love and marriage in a kind of
off-hand parenthesis, and then shown her what really
stood in the way: the awkwardness of Hop's looking so
unmistakably a Lambert. That was why they all wanted
her to part with him.

"I could not do it," she whispered. "Even if it means
choosing between you. It's true that I have come to love
you, Grove. Only I *could not* abandon that little boy who
trusts me and thinks I am his mother."

"Of course you could not," he said at once. "I never
thought you would; I had nothing to do with this well-
meaning interference. You told me at Palfreys that there
wasn't a man in the world who could separate you from
Hop, and I always believe what you say. I know very well
that if anyone is abandoned it must be me. Yet I cannot
help hoping that you will marry me in spite of the disad-
vantages. Before we go any further, I had better make it
quite clear what they are."

He sat down beside her on the sofa, and she blinked at him through the stupid tears that had rushed up to sting her eyelids. Grove crossed his legs and gazed at his well-polished boots while he talked. His manner was detached and reasonable. He was doing everything to avoid an unfair attack on her emotions.

"If we marry, the law will regard both Hop and Sukey as my stepchildren, the children of your late husband. Because he is so extremely like Henry, and like my own father, there will certainly be a great deal of comment; so much that I think we shall be bound to produce some explanation for our close friends. I should be inclined to say that Hop is my son, that his mother was a lady I don't choose to name, and that I took full responsibility for him. You were a friend of my daughter; she introduced us and I saw at once that you were just the person to have charge of the child. In due course I fell in love. That is not so far from the truth, after all, and I think everyone who knows us well enough would believe it. Certainly those who know *you* cannot think of you as the heroine of a sordid intrigue.

"But the rest of the world is not likely to be so charitable. They will jump to the obvious and much more interesting conclusion that you were my mistress for several years during the lifetime of my first wife. They won't be able to do you any real harm—not the sort of harm they could still do to Eliza; she could be ruined, even now, if it was known she had a child before she was married. You were already married when Hop was born, so you won't be ostracised. In fact many of the great ladies are more likely to include you in their own easy-going sisterhood. I'm afraid you won't care for that distraction. In the slightly lower ranks of society there will be a great deal of disapproval, but no actual snubs: the title will preserve you from those. And there you have it: there will be no real hardships to bear, but if you marry me you will lose the reputation you have always taken for granted and deserved, you will know that you are being gossiped about behind your back, you will sometimes encounter veiled insolence, and I shan't be able to defend you. All because of the kindness you once showed to a young girl in distress. It's a damnable injustice, and many people would say that I have no right to offer you marriage on such humiliating terms, I'm sure Henry will say so. No true romantic could endure to cast the shadow of scandal on his wife's good name. . . . I am not a romantic, Diana; I am just a man in love, longing for the real happiness I know I could share with you, that I never found completely with anyone before. Am I asking too much?"

"Do you suppose I care what strangers say about me, if I can be always with you and the children? What a craven you must think me," she exclaimed.

"I think you are almost too brave and generous, my lovely girl," said Grove, taking her in his arms. "But I shan't complain."

It was strange and delightful to be in love again, to kiss and be kissed, to feel the beat of his heart, the texture of his skin, to sense the deep desire behind an enquiring gentleness that put her pleasure before his own.

"How I long to see you at Paraden," he said presently. "That is where we shall live, you know: my favourite house. I can imagine you coming down the beautiful curved staircase, under the light from the cupola."

"Tell me about Paraden."

It was in the Grecian style, he said, quite unlike Brandham. Space and proportion were everything. He was planting an arboretum of rare trees in the park, and there was a lake and a trout stream and a temple fitted up as an observatory. The sea was not far off and there was a snug little harbour in the estuary where he kept his yacht.

All this talk of the garden and the sea made him want to go out—she had noticed he could not bear to be indoors in fine weather. The first people they saw in the Edenworth garden were Sukey and Francis, playing among the green shoots at the foot of one of the big trees in the avenue. An under-nursemaid was watching them from a distance.

Sukey came running up in her blue check gingham, her sun bonnet hanging by the strings.

"Mama! Mr. Wood!"

"He's not Mr. Wood," said Francis, following her. "He's my Uncle Grove."

Sukey was inclined to argue, and as Diana did not think this was the moment to explain Mr. Wood's double identity, she asked what they were doing.

"Playing mothers and fathers."

"That is a very good game to play," said Grove, catching Diana's eye. "Your mama is going to bring you and Hop to stay in my house, Sukey. Shall you like that?"

"Yes, please. Can we go now?"

When she heard they could not start at once, Sukey was a little disappointed and retired with Francis into their leafy home. They were soon having a very lifelike domestic squabble.

"I'm afraid Francis is going to be henpecked," said Grove.

Peels of laughter and a familiar creaking sound drew him and Diana towards the tree where the children had their swing. Henry, with his coat off, was pushing Hop and Charley, who sat side by side on the broad seat, each holding one of the ropes.

"Good afternoon, Mrs. Pentland," said Henry politely. "You can see I am making myself useful."

"How did you find Frank?" asked his father.

"Getting on pretty well, I think, sir. I sat with him for half an hour and then Maria said he'd talked enough. She's up there now."

There appeared to be no trace of strain, no lingering

awkwardness. That fortunate accident had shaken them all out of their conventional roles.

"You're the kite man," said Hop, who had been studying Grove.

"Quite right, young Hop."

"Why does he call you that?" asked Henry.

"It's a long story; I'll tell you someday. In the meantime I have some good news for you: I am going to marry Mrs. Pentland."

"I am very glad to hear it, sir. I hope you will both be very happy."

Henry looked and sounded genuinely pleased. It was extraordinary, Diana thought, how anxious the Lamberts and Desmonds were to further the marriage. Were they under the delusion that she would be able to manage his lordship for them? She was pretty sure they were wrong. Any managing that went on in Grove's vicinity he would do himself. She thought of Mr. Caversham and his Noble Client.

"What will happen to the boy?" asked Henry.

Grove glanced down at Hop, who had now got off the swing and was wrestling with Charley. Their conversation was literally above his head.

"We shall take the boy to Paraden with us, along with his sister."

Henry seemed doubtful. "I suppose you have considered—"

"Yes, we have considered," Grove answered, a little repressively.

Diana was afraid that Henry was going to annoy his father by stating some rather priggish views which Grove had already dismissed.

She said, "Your father has paid me a great compliment, Henry. May I call you that now? He has allowed me to decide my own fate, regardless of the pitfalls. Very few men will do that. They shelter women from every harsh wind that blows, and in doing so often compel us to lead ignorant, artificial lives and to behave like children. That is why so many of us become perfectly insipid. If I had sunk to that condition, I dare say I should be too frightened to accept a position in which I must be a target for speculation. I should have felt it necessary to refuse him —but even then I should have made up my own mind to run away. He would not take the decision for me."

"I can't imagine your ever being insipid, or running away," said Henry, surprised into gallantry. He flushed, looking quickly at his father, and seemed to regain some lost ground, for he smiled and said, "At least there is one shocking disclosure you will be able to avoid, sir."

This amused Grove. He told Henry not to be impudent, while sounding rather pleased.

Diana was mystified. What was the shocking disclosure? They could not be laughing about the secret that had caused Eliza so much anguish.

Grove enlightened her. "Henry has just pointed out, my love, that so long as everyone believes our small friend there is my son, nobody will guess he is my grandson."

It was an extraordinary thought. And very reassuring to find that Grove did not at all mind mentioning it. He was too much of a realist to suffer from pointless vanity, and he was plainly delighted to find that Henry was learning to speak his language, able to see the lighter side of their predicament instead of being solemn about it.

There were other aspects. The hopeless tangle of Hop's relationships. The presence within the family circle of both his natural parents; would they ever become possessive or try to interfere? And how would he and Sukey be affected by the gossip, once they were old enough to take it in? It was no use worrying about such things. Life was not a puzzle you could solve in advance. Diana slipped her hand through Grove's arm and felt a marvellous surge of happiness.

Hop had gone back to sit on the swing. Henry began lazily to push him, not too far, taking care that he didn't fall. The likeness between them was very strong, though Henry was probably less aware of it than anyone else, and Hop, of course, would not see it at all. Confidingly, without any special consciousness, he accepted the labours of the useful man pushing the swing: the unacknowledged uncle who was about to become his stepbrother.